FLAMES AND FRYING PANS

KATE MOSEMAN

Cover by ArcaneCovers.com

ISBN 978-1-957320-17-5 (ebook)

ISBN 978-1-957320-24-3 (paperback)

Fortunella Press

For all the fans,
because you kept me going

1

I'm trying to show Jessica—for the third time—how to slice tomatoes correctly, and it's rapidly becoming one of those moments when I regret ninety percent of my life choices.

"You like sharp things, Jessica," I said. "How can you possibly be so incompetent at using a knife?"

"I like using sharp things on *people*. How can you blame me if tomatoes don't hold my interest?" She tried again. Half the slice you could see through. Half the slice was as thick as a Zagat guidebook.

"Just give it to me." I grabbed the tomato and did it myself, wondering whatever possessed me to accept Jessica's oath of loyalty, and why I ever thought training her at the restaurant would be a good way of instilling discipline that wasn't bloodsucking-related. "Go roll silverware."

"Yes, Zelda." Her little curtsy was perfectly correct and also made me want to smack her face.

"James!" I called out.

My other vampire kitchen assistant—the competent one—looked up from monitoring the hot breakfast sandwiches.

"Are we ready?"

"Ready, boss."

"Let's go." We swung into action: wrapping, bagging, passing everything off to Lily, who sorted out the orders and the money before the morning customers scooped up their prizes and hustled out the door. Every time the door opened, cold air swirled in, a reminder that summer was behind us.

James, Lily, and I danced through the rest of the rush. Jessica found a niche in rolling silverware and occasionally taking to the floor with a broom with an industriousness that surprised me. When the open fire hydrant of customers finally weakened to a trickle, we were in good shape, with time enough to get ready for the next rush. Lily disappeared to the back to check supplies, and James went to work on cleaning up the kitchen.

I checked the morning's receipts and allowed myself a satisfied nod. Not bad. Not bad at all. I wouldn't be a millionaire anytime soon, but West Side Sandwiches was making it. Grandma would be proud. The occupational license with her embellishment, *West Side 'Wiches* instead of *West Side Sandwiches*, had some smudges on it, so I scrubbed it down with a clean towel. "There," I said, nudging the frame so it would hang exactly straight. "That's better."

I'd added framed pictures around it: me and Poppy at Central Park; Lily holding Jester; and a very old photo of the one time my mom came with me to New York, when I was a kid, to see Grandma. That one was so old the colors were washed out.

No photos of Berron or Daniel, yet. But I used Daniel's knife every day, and every time I wiped down the wooden bar or the tabletops, I was reminded of Berron. Beautiful and useful things were always my weakness.

Jessica appeared behind me with the stealth of a ghost. "Why didn't you put *Daniel* to work? He's your Initiate, too."

"Because Daniel has a job, and you don't. You've been out of the workplace since the nineties. Consider this your retraining program."

Jessica sniffed. "I was an art major."

"Very practical of you." I didn't have anything against pursuing dreams—hell, Lily was a fashion major, and I'd opened the type of business rated most likely to fail in the first year—but I wasn't going to let her sniff at me. "Floor needs mopping."

She flounced off.

I could have used a second cup of coffee. Instead, the bells jangled, and someone came through the door with another blast of cold autumn air, a relief from the heat of the grill. I was momentarily blinded by the flash of sunlight. While I was still blinking, the door swung closed, and I heard a familiar Southern voice.

"Zelda, girl!"

I rubbed my eyes. Surely I wasn't seeing right. Short, fluffy hair. Wide smile. Sparkling, expressive eyes. Posture so straight you could almost be fooled into thinking she wasn't actually petite.

And she was carrying a suitcase.

"*Mom?*"

My mother laughed, lightly, but with an edge of nervousness. "I thought I'd come try this new restaurant I heard about."

Seeing my mom standing in West Side Sandwiches was like ordering a hot dog from a street cart and having them hand you a live marmoset instead. "You flew up from Florida? Why didn't you *call* me?"

Mom moved hesitantly through the tables and chairs, her free hand tracing the seatbacks as she went. "I thought I'd surprise you! Isn't that fun?"

What do you even *do* with a live marmoset? I mean, I suppose it *was* fun, in a way, but maybe not ideal, for various reasons.

Also confusing. My mom didn't do surprises, and was in fact one of the least surprising people I'd ever known. Mom had *predictable* down to an art. "Yeah!" I said. "That's—um—fantastic." I sounded like an idiot and I knew it. "Did you eat yet?" I said, falling back on creaky old Southern manners out of sheer panic.

"Oh, I don't want to put you to any trouble—"

"Aunt Effie!" Lily cried. She rushed forward and threw her arms around my mom. "Zelda didn't say you were coming to visit!"

"Zelda didn't know she was coming to visit," I muttered to myself.

James came out from behind the counter and introduced himself. "Ma'am, I am so pleased to meet you. There are so many stories I could tell you about your daughter—"

I cleared my throat.

"But I'm sure you'll want to hear them directly from her. Can I get you something? Coffee? Tea? Eggs? I do a mean omelet." He pulled out a chair and ushered her into it.

"An omelet would be lovely." She put a hand on his arm. "Do you have Cracker Barrel extra sharp cheese?" James looked blank. "Never mind, whatever you have will be fine, I'm sure." She patted his arm reassuringly.

James retreated, no doubt in search of the mythical Cracker Barrel extra sharp.

I tried to think of a good way of asking *why are you here* without just shouting it. Nothing came to mind. So I went sideways. "Do you have a place to stay?"

"I expect there's a Holiday Inn or something around here. Or a bed and breakfast"—she looked at Lily—"I love a good B&B, don't you?"

Lily nodded happily. Of course she did. It wasn't *her* mother showing up out of nowhere.

"I mean, if you'd have *called* me—"

Mom waved the thought away. "I didn't want to stress you out."

"So you came *here* to stress me out?"

That earned me a well-deserved look. "I came," she said, "to see my *daughter*."

I looked at her more closely, as if I could see a clue in the lines of her face. If she wanted to travel, why hadn't she gone to my brother's? She had always seemed to approve of him more than me.

Why was she *here?* "Lily," I said, "could you check in the produce delivery?"

Lily hesitated, her gaze going back and forth between my mom and me, before she disappeared into the back again.

I leaned toward Mom, ready to get the full truth, when I caught Jessica, out of the corner of my eye, using the mopping as a pretense to skulk closer and closer. "Jessica, go help Lily."

Jessica huffed a sigh and marched off, nearly mowing down James, who was carrying a plate.

"Watch it," he said. Then he put on a smile and delivered the omelet to our table. "Cheddar cheese omelet, ma'am. Enjoy." He leaned close to me. "I'll keep everything under control," he murmured.

"Thank you, James," I said. Mom just sat there, looking oddly guilty, like Jester when I busted him with a mouthful of scrunchies. "Mom. Your omelet?"

Mom started, then daintily unrolled the silverware and laid the napkin across her lap. "I'm fine, really."

"I never said you *weren't* fine."

"Well, I am." She stabbed the eggs with her fork.

I waited.

Mom chewed and swallowed, looking anywhere but at me. Then she laid down her fork. "Stop looking at me like that."

"Like what?"

"Like you're waiting for me to confess."

I slid into a seat across from her. "No offense, Mom, but this isn't like you. You don't just pick up and travel on the spur of the moment." *To a city you don't even like*, I could have added.

She took another bite of omelet, then waved the fork around. "Isn't it enough that I want to see my daughter?"

I raised an eyebrow.

"Oh, all right. Fine." She leaned in. "I'm getting older, Zelda. I feel like..." She shifted uncomfortably before continuing. "I feel like we're not as close as we should be. And—maybe if we spent some *time* together, I don't know..."

"So you just—" I made my hand into an airplane and flew it through the space between us.

"Yes," she said, her voice turning firmer. More familiar. "Yes, I did. Your Aunt Belinda said she had a wonderful time up here with you and Lily, and so I thought to myself, 'Why not, Effie? Before you're too old for such foolishness?'"

"You've never been foolish."

"Maybe I should have been."

I looked at her and our gazes struck like two stock pots colliding, hard enough to ring your ears and vibrate your bones. My wild, secret hope—that she would sensibly decide to hop on a plane and go home—vanished.

I had always known we were both stubborn.

I had never known we were both prone to bold, reckless moves. It goes to show that people you've known all your life can still surprise you. "I'm glad you came," I said, finally. "In fact," I continued, swallowing my misgivings, "you can stay with Poppy and me. You can have my room. I'll take the couch."

"Oh, no," Mom said. She looked down and fiddled with her napkin. "I couldn't possibly put you on the couch."

"I insist."

She raised her gaze to mine. "Really?"

"Really."

She perked up. "Thank you, honey." Genuine gratitude, but also a faint hint of triumph. "I'll just—enjoy the changing of the season," she said, gesturing to the air as if leaves were turning inside the restaurant. "I won't be any trouble, I promise."

Trouble. I'd dealt with a never-ending run of it since coming to New York. What was a little visit from my mom?

No trouble. No trouble at all.

2

Mom stood on the sidewalk outside Poppy's and stared up at the stone townhouse. "Oh, my. This is *elegant*." She leaned in conspiratorially and lowered her voice. "Does your friend come from money?"

"Mom!" I should have remembered that my mother observed signs of social status like some people watch birds. Not with judgment, but with encyclopedic fascination.

"What? There's no shame in it."

"She's from England."

My mother's hand flew to her chest with happy shock, probably from one too many episodes of Masterpiece Theater. "Is she a peer?"

"*Please* don't ask her that."

Mom lifted her chin. "Do I look like a barbarian?"

"Yes. A tiny Southern librarian-barbarian. Come on, Jester's waiting for us."

My ridiculous miniature poodle had popped up in the window, head cocked and ears perked, alert to my arrival—and the arrival of someone new, whose face probably needed to be kissed. When I opened the door, he rushed us, going up on two legs and bouncing excitedly, tongue flying this way and that.

"Jester! Jester, sit," I said, as he attempted to jump even higher. "Hold on, Mom." I pulled a treat out and waved it at him. "Sit, you idiot."

Jester sat, quivering, eyes shining, tail wagging even when it could only scoot back and forth on the floor.

"Good boy." I tossed him the treat and scooped him up in a practiced motion, hoping he'd calm the heck down. "Say hello to Mom."

Jester craned his neck toward my mom, licking his own nose in an attempt to give her doggy kisses.

She scratched his head. "He's so soft, he doesn't even feel like a dog."

"Well, he thinks he's human, so that makes sense."

A door opened and shut upstairs, followed by the sounds of footsteps and heavy paws on the stairs. Poppy and Georgiana emerged into the living room. "Zelda! You're home early," Poppy said.

"Mom, this is my friend, Poppy, and her Irish wolfhound, Georgiana. Poppy, this is my mom, Effie."

My mom held out her hand. "So nice to meet you, Poppy."

Bright curiosity bloomed on Poppy's face. "Hello!" she said, shaking Mom's hand and then quickly moving back. "Does she—um—*know*?"

"Oh, right. Mom, Poppy reads minds. If you're within about six feet of her, she can see what you're thinking."

My mother's dazzling smile froze, then faltered. "*Does* she? How unique!" She clutched her bag and retreated to the couch, where she set the bag aside and began to feel the couch with her hands. "Is this the couch you were talking about sleeping on?"

"The one and only."

"I can't possibly do that to you. You have all that work on you. You simply must get your sleep."

"I'll be fine—"

"No, no, no. I won't impose on your hospitality. I'll find a nice little place to stay nearby."

"Actually," Poppy said, "the LWW has a few rooms open right now. I'm sure I could arrange a complimentary stay."

"The what now?" Mom asked.

"LWW," I said. "League of Women's Welfare. A local charity with a great big beautiful building in the Upper East Side."

"You don't mind hanging out with a lot of witches, do you?" Poppy said.

"Witches?" Mom swallowed. "Do they... read minds, too?" It was one thing to know that magic made Mom uncomfortable. It was another thing to watch it happen in real time. Most of the time we mutually pretended the problem didn't exist.

"Not like me," Poppy replied, breezily. "I can't help it. They have to do it intentionally." She leaned down to Georgiana and gave the Irish wolfhound scritchy-scratchies behind her ears. "Isn't that right, girl?" she said. "I'm a great big mind-reading monster."

Mom shifted, her discomfort at being impolite obviously warring with the desire not to have her mind read.

Poppy looked up. "I'd be happy to talk to Azure."

"She's the boss witch lady," I added.

"Witch Presiding," Poppy said. "I'm sure we could get you a lovely room for your stay."

"Oh, no," my mother said, looking alarmed, "I wouldn't want you to go to any trouble."

Jester jumped on the couch and threw himself across her lap. He did that when people needed comforting. Then he rolled over and showed his belly, hoping for tummy rubs.

"Well, aren't you a demanding boy?" she said.

"Speaking of which," I said, "I'm supposed to meet up with Berron."

"Berron?"

In my mind, I had to run through what she knew and didn't know. About Berron, not much. "He helped me renovate, remember?"

"Oh, yes." She paused. "What is Daniel doing these days? Such a nice boy," she added.

Poppy barely covered a snort-laugh by coughing.

My mom continued. "Maybe you two should get back together again—"

Poppy's cough turned into full-blown pneumonia.

"Men," I said, with a hard look at Poppy, "are a fun distraction. Like Oreo cookies. They're good, but you can't plan your life around them."

"Life without Oreos wouldn't be as sweet, Zelda," Mom countered.

"Oh, look at the time!" I glanced at my watch-less wrist, then moved to give her a hug. "I have to go out."

Mom shied away, causing Jester to flip right-side-up in surprise. "I think I'm a little under the weather," she said. "Wouldn't want you to catch anything."

"Oh." I lowered my arms, backed away. This reunion had been six kinds of awkward already. "Well. Make yourself at home. Rest in my room. There's food in the fridge if you want it. Unless you'd rather Poppy set you up at witch headquarters..."

"I'd rather stay with you," she said quickly. "You're sure you don't mind?"

"Of course not. I'll see you later." I gave her a wave instead of a hug.

Jester bolted off the couch and down the hall, thinking I'd thrown something fun, and Georgiana ambled after him.

I sighed. "Could you get them a treat, Poppy?"

"Treat time!" Poppy called to the dogs.

I turned back to Mom. She had always been petite, but she looked smaller than I remembered. When did that happen? She was always so sure of herself, especially when she was disapproving of my life choices, or of magic in general.

I didn't say any of that, though.

I just told her I loved her, and left.

When the vines overgrew the buildings in Gramercy Park, the media called it *an unusual climatological event.*

I called it a pain in the butt, because the only way to make the new growth retreat was to communicate with each plant, personally, and ask it to go back to where it came from. And of course Berron and I were the only two beings who could do this job—Berron, because it was his type of magic and the rest of the Gentry didn't dig running around Manhattan—and me, because I could copy his magic.

But before I could lay hands on the plants, I had to lay hands on him.

Professionally speaking.

Except I was at Gramercy Square, and he wasn't. No sign of the tall Gentry prince. *Where are you?* I texted.

Union Square Greenmarket, he replied.

"Union Square! That's three blocks from where you're supposed to be," I said aloud, looking at my phone with annoyance that Berron, unfortunately, couldn't see.

There's a new bread vendor, he added.

"You think you can soothe me with bread?" I scoffed to myself.

He could, and he knew it. Damn him.

I punched in a reply—*Fine, I'm coming*—shoved my phone in my pocket, and walked.

My breath puffed out in clouds in the cold air. November could get cold in Florida, sure, but it was nothing like the consistent chill of an NYC autumn, the kind that climbed up from the concrete sidewalks. I'd had to re-learn how to layer to stay warm: good socks, Doc Martens, jeans, a thermal undershirt, black turtleneck, and a hip-length navy peacoat. A fuzzy ski hat with pom-pom topper—a gift from Poppy, who made them in her spare time—kept the heat in like a pot lid.

By the time I reached Union Square, the walk had made me even warmer than I needed to be, so I stripped off the hat and unbuttoned my coat.

As annoyed as I'd been at having to walk three blocks out of the way, it all faded away as soon as I entered the farmers market.

Pop-up tents on all sides. Stacks of purple, orange, and white carrots four feet high. Fresh-cut flower bouquets, studded with pine cones, wrapped in brown paper, and spilling out of buckets and baskets. Jugs of freshly-pressed apple cider. Piles of winter squash: green, white, yellow, and gold.

And then, the bread.

Bread everywhere. Ciabatta and bagels and rustic peasant loaves. Sourdough and buckwheat and pretzel twists. Not to mention sweeter baked goods like pies and lemon-blueberry pound cakes.

I had stopped to look closer—purely business interest—when the scent of forests and rain blended with the almost steamy aroma of freshly-baked bread, and a warm presence loomed behind my shoulder.

"I knew you'd want some," Berron said.

"Yeah, yeah, like it takes a genius to know I love bread." I took my time turning around, only to find him waving a hot soft pretzel at me, studded with gems of salt.

He took a bite and rolled his eyes in a dramatic show of ecstasy, moaning aloud to really drive home the effect.

"Give me that." I seized his wrist and pulled the pretzel closer, pulling Berron closer, too. Gave me a better look at his corduroy blazer, thick multicolored knitted scarf—Poppy again—and the cranberry felt fedora perched at a rakish angle on his dark locks.

He looked good and he knew it.

I tore a hunk of pretzel off with my teeth.

"Like it?"

"Mm," I said, shortly, not willing to show how much I liked it. We walked on, passing the pretzel back and forth.

"They make really good sourdough, too. Hundred-year-old mother."

I laughed. "Older than mine. She showed up today, by the way. Out of nowhere. Said she wanted to 'visit.'"

"'Showed up'? As in *here*?"

"Yes, here. At the shop. She's going to stay with Poppy and me."

"Is she on vacation or something?"

"Oh, no, nothing that normal. She just decided to show up... and here she is."

"I thought you two weren't that close."

"We love each other, but we're just so *different*." I shook my head, shook away the thoughts. "We should get back to Gramercy Park."

"What's the rush?" He gestured toward the market, a move that seemed to encompass all the baked goods that could be sampled and shared.

"'What's the rush?'" I punched his arm. "Let's just let those plants overgrow everything. That's not suspicious at *all*."

Berron shrugged. "So there's plants on the buildings. So what?"

"Green plants halfway to winter draw attention, especially when they're literally climbing the walls. You don't want attention. You want to stay hidden in your nice pocket universe, not have a bunch of maniacs trying to exploit it or take it over or burn it down."

Berron's brow contracted, and his lower lip edged slightly out.

"Why are you pouting?" I said.

" I wish—"

"You wish what?"

"I wish it were different. Everything green in this city is hemmed in. No one grows anything here. When you want real food you have to have it trucked in from hours away."

"What do you want, a farm? The days when Sheep Meadow was actually a meadow filled with sheep are long gone."

Berron stopped at an organic apple-seller. He picked up a large, red apple. "I want to see the tree this came from. I want to lie down under the shade of its branches. I want to drink from the stream that watered it and I want to pick the fruit with my own hands."

The apple-seller came over. "You gonna buy that or are you just gonna wave it around?"

Berron looked annoyed at being interrupted, before reaching into his pocket for cash. He bit into the apple as we walked on, then wordlessly passed it to me.

I took it, bit into the unbitten side. Apple skin snapped crisply beneath my teeth and sweet juice fizzed onto my lips. "You have that," I said. "Just not here." I handed the apple back to him.

"I want both," he said.

We continued walking, leaving the Union Square Greenmarket behind for Park Avenue, where it led north-northeast.

What got me about our impromptu trip to the greenmarket was how very *normal* it was. He wasn't calling me *my Zelda* anymore, and he'd stopped proposing to make me his queen. But when he looked at me, sometimes—when he thought I wasn't looking—I still could see that glint in his eye. Veiled, but there all the same. Even over bites of apple he was still doing it.

Could I tell him to stop looking at me that way?

Did I *want* to?

When we reached Gramercy Park, I surveyed what was left of the work we had done. The vines that had overgrown the buildings had mostly backed down, due to our maintenance and probably due to the cold, as well. But new growth lurked in crevices, green and tentative, waiting for a chance to climb again.

I stopped and leaned against the black rails of the fence surrounding the private park. "Are you ready?"

"Of course." He took his hands out of his jacket pockets and held them out.

I removed my hands from my pockets, and before the cold air could chill them, took Berron's hands in mine. To any outsider we would have looked like a couple. We weren't. We were friends. Friends who had kissed a couple of times, sure. And maybe he had tried to make me his queen, once. But all that had happened when his whole world needed saving.

Everything was resolved, now. This was just... the cleanup. This was business.

Probably should have looked away when the magic started.

Instead, his gaze held me in place, pinned to the bars of the fence, while green and gold vines spiraled around my hands, sinking into my flesh with a sigh that whispered of enchanted forests.

It means nothing, I reminded myself, over and over again until it was like a mantra: *nothing, nothing, nothing*, while his eyes were shadows in the forest, hiding mysteries.

I had the magic. I could let go. And yet I wanted to hold on longer, even as I had to let go before it became obvious. I gasped at the shock of disconnection, quickly covering it with a cough.

It was just magic.

It meant nothing.

3

We made our way around the outside of the park itself, strolling and casually pausing to whisper to wayward vines. I was investigating a tiny vine wrapped around a carriage light when a familiar presence entered my perception like the scent of toast reaching peak golden-brown. I turned, knowing who I would see, knowing he would be outlined in red, like banked coals waiting for a breath.

"Daniel," I said. "What are you doing here?"

He stood before me dressed to the nines as usual. Beautifully draped slacks over fine leather shoes. Trench coat layered over suit and tie. He turned and pointed up. "I saw you from the window."

The picture window facing the park, in Prospero's apartment. Of course. "Cleaning it out?"

His eyebrows rose. "Why would I clean it out?"

Berron, who had been kneeling to inspect the sidewalk a short distance away, rose and approached.

"To sell it," I said.

"Sell what?" Berron asked. He nodded cordially to Daniel, who raised his chin in greeting.

"Prospero's apartment," I answered.

"Oh, right." Berron nodded.

"Who said I was selling anything?" Daniel said.

Cue the record scratch. My mouth opened, and for once, I couldn't think of anything to say.

Berron smiled like it was Christmas and his birthday all at once. "You're keeping it?"

"Daniel," I said. "You almost *died* there. Why would you want to keep it?"

He rubbed one hand over his head, looking less like the Lord of the Blessed and more like a boy caught with his hand in the pickle jar. "I thought Jessica might like her old room back, you know? And it gets her out of Victorine's hair."

This was accurate, thoughtful, and also suspicious. I'd known Daniel long enough to know that. So I waited. One of the best ways to get people to talk is to just shut up.

Berron wouldn't have looked out of place with a tub of popcorn, the way he was watching Daniel and me.

"Besides, I like the building. It has style," Daniel said.

I kept waiting.

"I could even sell my own condo, you know—"

"*What?*" My breath blew out like dragon smoke. "You're moving in? You're moving into *Prospero's apartment*? With *Jessica*? Are you insane?" I got right up to Daniel's chest and poked a finger in his silk tie. "She nearly killed you!"

He shrugged. "I'm not afraid of her."

"I'm not afraid of her, either." Not strictly true. I still wondered what she was capable of. "But it's different," I said.

How *was* it different, though? I'd kept her around; kept her close, even, working at the restaurant. And on the face of it, he was doing the same.

But he *wasn't*. I was sure of it.

I just couldn't describe it in a way that made sense.

Berron's obvious delight was distracting. I threw up my hands. "Fine. Shack up with Jessica. Who am I to tell 'Lord' Daniel what to do?"

"I still outrank you, by the way," Berron said.

"And yet here you are," Daniel replied, "cleaning up my sidewalk."

"Are you two done?" I said.

"As you wish, my—" Berron stopped, cleared his throat. My name hung in the air unsaid. "*My*, what a lovely day."

I was about to respond when I heard something in the distance. Something jingling. A high chime like tiny bells carved from crystal.

Ice cream truck, I thought. *It's only an ice cream truck.*

In the fall, though?

They were both staring at me. Daniel waved at me. "Zelda? You okay?"

"I'm fine." *Ice cream truck, ice cream truck, ice cream truck.* If I kept thinking it, that would make it so. Or it would have, if a scent hadn't slipped between the everpresent exhaust, the nearby green and growing plants, and the lingering taste of apple on my lips.

Star fruit.

Berron had his hand on my shoulder. I hadn't even noticed him put it there. "Hey," he said, giving me a shake. "You zoned out on us."

"It's nothing." They looked doubtful. "What? I can't stop and think for a minute?"

"No offense," Daniel said, "but it's really not like you."

"Shut up," I said. But on the inside, I seized the memory of their embrace, the one that held me together as I reflected the magic of the Arcade, and wrapped it around me like a warm blanket to stop the chill crawling over my arms. A chill that had nothing to do with the season.

And just like that, the scent of star fruit faded away as if I'd only imagined it.

"Why don't you guys come up?" Daniel said.

"Hm?" I said, barely coming back to the present in time to register what Daniel had said. "Oh." I glanced up, toward Prospero's window. No—*Daniel's* window. The change was too bizarre. "Sure," I said.

We walked back to Daniel's building.

Outside, there was still a gap in the hedge where Berron had pulled up a shrub and used it to restrain Jessica when we ran off with the stolen Mirror. Poor Mirror. So beautiful, now smashed into a million pieces. Not knowing what else to do, Poppy and I had swept them up and put them in a box in a closet for safekeeping, along with the empty frame.

We squeezed into the too-small elevator together, only to have Berron lunge for the doors and slip out just before they closed. "Be right back," he called.

The door slid shut, and our body heat made the air temperature rise even as the elevator did. I exhaled when the doors opened and we stepped into the cooler, darker hallway.

Daniel led the way to his door, wielding a key before turning the handle and letting the door swing wide. "Come on in."

We stepped inside. I shrugged off my jacket, removed my scarf, and tossed both over the back of the nearest couch. I did a pretty good job of looking nonchalant, I think, even though being in Prospero's apartment still gave me the heebie-jeebies. Too many memories tinted red.

"It smells like someone's grandma lives here," I said.

"Dried flowers and a candy bowl," Daniel said, helpfully pointing to the relevant items. "I'll open a window." He unlatched one and pushed the sash upward. It slid into place with a creak.

Cold autumn air poured in. Prospero's apartment had always seemed hermetically sealed, like a time capsule—the Victorian dollhouse decor didn't help—but by opening a window, the modern world blew inside. "You gonna keep all this stuff?"

"Why not?" Daniel said.

"It's not exactly your style," I replied, thinking of his high-rise condo, sleek with glass and metal.

"Neither was drinking blood, Zelda, but we all have to adapt."

Berron burst through the unlocked door carrying an uprooted plant. Dirt rained down on the oriental carpet as he brandished the shrub. "I'm back!" His gaze swept the room and landed on a probably priceless porcelain Chinese urn decorated with painted goldfish. He dropped the shrub into the urn, poked at its drooping leaves and frowned, then cracked his knuckles.

Green and gold magic enveloped the plant. Healthy new growth doubled the length of the branches, and spring green leaves unfurled. Tiny flower buds appeared, grew, then burst open with pink petals and a fresh, delicate scent. "Ta-da!" Berron said, gesturing to the rosebush. "Housewarming present."

I moved closer to examine the roses, and found an old book sitting next to the pot. I picked up the book and read the title aloud: "'Manners for Men.'" Then I flipped a few pages. "Published in 1897. Oh, listen to this: 'Woman's Ideal Man.' This ought to be good."

"Pray continue," Berron said, throwing himself down on one of the sofas.

I cleared my throat. "'I suppose there was never yet a woman who had not somewhere set up on a pedestal in her brain an ideal of manhood. He is by no means immutable, this paragon. On the contrary, he changes very often.'"

"See?" Daniel interrupted. "'Changes very often.'"

"Be quiet, I'm not done reading. 'Like every other woman, I have my ideal of manhood. The difficulty is to describe it. First of all, he must be a gentleman'—"

"Simplicity itself." Berron lounged more comfortably and aimed a smirk at Daniel.

I read on. "'Gentleness and moral strength combined must be the salient characteristics of the gentleman... He must be thoughtful for others, kind to women and children and all helpless things, tender-hearted to the old and the poor and the unhappy, but never foolishly weak in giving where gifts do harm instead of good—his brain must be as fine as his heart, in fact.'"

"Ah, so much for Daniel, then," Berron said.

Daniel heaved a long-suffering sigh but didn't rise to the bait.

"'There are few such men,'" I continued, "'but they do exist. I know one or two. Reliable as rocks, judicious in every action, dependable in trifles as well as the large affairs of life, full of mercy and kindness to others, affectionate and well-loved in their homes, their lives are pure and kindly.'" I closed the book with a snap and dropped it back on the table.

Daniel and Berron traded a dubious expression. "'Pure and kindly'?" Daniel said.

"That might be going a little *too* far," Berron agreed.

I snatched up embroidered pillows and threw one at each of them. Berron simply caught his one-handed in mid-air, while Daniel caught his in both hands and flung it back at me.

I dodged. "Missed me."

"What else is in here, anyway?" Berron said. He glided from lounging to prowling, followed by opening and closing drawers, looking behind picture frames, and chucking more pillows around as if to see if anything was hidden underneath. "There's got to be something interesting." He pulled a sword cane from the round stand and unsheathed it. Then he aimed it at the sofa.

"What the hell are you doing?" asked Daniel.

"Investigating," Berron said.

"Not on my couch, you're not."

Berron held eye contact with Daniel and punched the sharp point through the fabric. White clouds of stuffing burst from the slash.

"Dude, what is your problem?" He lunged at Berron, who—instead of whipping the blade back like a game of keep-away—simply aimed the point at Daniel. Daniel froze rather than be impaled.

"No problem," Berron said cheerfully. "No problem at all."

"Berron," I said, "put the sword away and stop wrecking the furniture."

"Bah." He re-sheathed it and dropped it back in the stand. "No one lets me have any fun."

Daniel examined the sofa's wound.

"Where's Jessica's room?" I said.

Daniel straightened. "Over there. Why? You want to punch holes in her furniture, too?"

"*I* didn't punch holes in *anything*. Mr. Gentry Prince did that."

Berron grinned.

I walked toward the door of Jessica's room.

"Wait," Daniel said. "You can't just go through her stuff."

"Who said I was going through her stuff?" That had been exactly what I was going to do, in fact, but I was willing to be flexible. "I just want to see what her room looks like." Before he could protest any more, I turned the heavy knob and opened the door.

A heavy mahogany bed frame nearly filled the room. A vanity table with small drawers and a mirror sat to one side. A tall folding screen stood in the opposite corner. It looked as if dozens of cut-outs from Victorian prints had been glazed onto the panels: roses, Queen Victoria, Prince Albert, a child with a dog. Swans and battle scenes and bowls of fruit. Carriages and pretty ladies. One of the strangest pieces of furniture I'd ever seen.

I stepped into the room with Daniel on my heels, followed by Berron.

Her vanity table held black eyeliner, black mascara, red lipstick, and a dark, almost apple-shaped bottle of perfume. I picked up the perfume. "Poison," I said, gazing at the familiar bottle, one that had sat on many a bathroom counter in the nineties. "That's almost *too* obvious."

Berron took the bottle from my hand, uncapped it, and spritzed it into the air.

"Stop it," Daniel said. "She'll know you were in here."

Berron, unbothered, sniffed the air. "She'll think *you* were in here."

I waved a hand in front of my face. "My God, I'd forgotten that smell."

"You don't like it?" Berron said.

I wrinkled my nose. "Spilled grape soda and cinnamon? No, thanks."

Berron peered at the bottle. "For something called 'Poison,' it's awfully sweet."

"Great," Daniel said, taking the bottle from Berron's hand. "We've all had our fun, now let's go back to the living room."

"How about Prospero's room?" I said.

"Daniel's room," Berron corrected.

Daniel shot him a look. "Sure. Anything that will get you out of here."

"Lead on," I said, the perfume still tickling my nose.

We left Jessica's Poison-scented Victorian boudoir behind.

Prospero's bedroom door was exactly the same, but inside, everything was different. The larger space permitted a thick Persian rug on the floor. Prospero had a dark wooden bed frame, but this one had high columns and curtains like it belonged to Ebenezer Scrooge. A matching dresser next to an old Victrola phonograph. In place of a vanity table, there were bookshelves filled with volumes decorated with gold lettering on the spines. And instead of a screen, Prospero had a marble fireplace with a mirror hanging above the mantel.

I passed through the doorway and rested my hand on one of the bed columns. In a strange way, it was similar to my own room—poster bed, fireplace, bookshelves—but dark and stuffy where mine glowed with sunlight. "Are you actually going to sleep in here?" I pictured Daniel's bedroom, where all the wood was light-colored and Scandinavian smooth, and the sheets were the latest high-tech fabric.

"I already do," he said.

And I nodded as if it was nothing, while I wondered if ghosts would haunt his dreams.

4

Berron ransacked the chest of drawers while Daniel half crawled under the bed, looking for anything of interest. I knelt by the fireplace and summoned Patty Melt, my fire mouse. Maybe a fire could banish the presence of dead vampire lords.

She popped into my hand with a hiss like a sparkler igniting. I put my hand close to the logs that had already been neatly laid in the grate with old newspaper tucked into the wood. The seasoned wood had laid untouched since the summer, waiting for autumn—and a master who would never return. "Go on, hop down," I said.

Patty Melt's whiskers twitched like burning threads.

"Look at all that nice paper. Don't you want to burn it up?"

Patty took hesitant steps forward, her tiny claws like hot fork tines. Then she ambled onto the logs, seized a twist of newspaper, and began chewing on it. Smoke rose from the wood where she sat.

"Good girl," I said.

Berron tossed items over his shoulder. Bow ties and socks rained down. "Boring. Boring. Boring. *Double* boring."

Daniel slid out from under the bed frame and brushed the way-ward accessories from where they'd landed on his legs and torso. "Nothing under there."

"Stay in the fireplace," I told Patty. Then I stood up, dodging more flying socks, and moved to the closet. I opened the door. Prospero's suits hung neatly from thick wooden hangers.

Daniel joined me. "The man had some nice threads."

I pulled a tweed jacket out. "Maybe we could donate them." But as my fingers grazed the richly textured cloth, I felt faintly sick. I should have been cool and calm, going through Prospero's things. He had, after all, trashed my shop, threatened all I held dear, and nearly destroyed the home of the Gentry.

"You're getting that faraway look again," Daniel said. "Are you all right?"

"I came here to make sandwiches," I said, quietly, tracing the curve of the jacket collar. "I never meant for any of this to happen."

"For what to happen?"

"I never meant to…" I stopped, remembering the biting cold, the flood of magic. Prospero's brittle bravery. It tasted of metal and ash, like I'd licked the fire grate. "I never meant for anyone to get hurt. Even someone as bad as Prospero."

Daniel's eyes glowed redder, enhanced by touches of orange from the fire. "He would have destroyed everything in his path until he got what he wanted. You don't have to feel guilty. Berron would say the same." He paused and looked over to where Berron was elbows-deep in another drawer. "Right, Berron?"

"Hm?"

"Back me up. Zelda shouldn't feel guilty for taking Prospero out."

"Of course she shouldn't. If she takes on the guilt for what he did, she's not giving him credit for the only good thing he tried to do."

My eyebrows rose so high I felt my hair shift. "The only *good* thing he tried to do? Destroying the Forest of Emeralds?"

Berron stopped rummaging and looked up. "I'm agreeing with you. Don't you like that?"

"Um, maybe *not...*"

"He did the wrong thing for the right reason. He sacrificed himself to free his people. I can't say I'd have done exactly the same thing, but I can understand why he did it." Berron carefully closed the drawer. He faced me, and his mahogany irises glittered with firelight. "Do you think you could have made a better choice? One that didn't end in Prospero hurling himself into the arms of the Arcade?"

I looked away, unable to speak.

He came closer and laid one hand on my cheek. Damn me, I closed my eyes and let him. "Regrets are a fire," he said, his voice gentle. "They light the way. But don't let them burn you down."

Green and gold magic bloomed behind my eyelids, nearly mesmerizing me, as his words wrapped me like a crocheted blanket. If only I could stay here, where nothing else existed but magic and warmth—

Except Daniel was pointedly clearing his throat, and the acrid scent of burning wool suddenly stung my nose. I opened my eyes and hurried to the fireplace, following a trail of scorch marks on the floor.

Patty Melt sat in the fire, contentedly munching on one of Prospero's socks.

"Patty!" How did you reprimand a fire mouse, anyway? I settled for sighing heavily. "If you get a tummy ache, Miss Patty, don't come running to me, you hear me?" I heard my mother's voice in my own words.

Which reminded me—

Mom. In my town. In my shop. I had more important things to do than this. I'd donate the clothing and move on.

And that would be the last of it.

I gathered Patty Melt into my hand, the heat of the fire no more than a caress of warmth, and removed the smoldering sock from her grasp. "Dunk this in some water, will you?" I said, handing it to Daniel. "All right, kid," I said, returning my attention to the fire mouse, who was yawning. "Sleep it off." I closed my other hand over her. Her warmth diffused through me, and I felt her presence return to where she slumbered in my mind.

"Okay," I said, standing up and putting my hands on my hips. "Pile all the clothing on the bed. I'll take it over to Lily. Maybe she and her fashion-forward friends can make use of it."

"How will you carry it all?" Daniel asked.

"Put it in the quilt and wrap it up. I'll throw it in a cab."

Berron met my gaze silently, for one beat too long, then turned away. He retrieved socks and bow ties from where they'd landed and tossed them into the center of the bed covering.

The finished bundle looked like we'd rolled up Cleopatra in a rug, but thanks to borrowed magic, I lifted it easily, refusing help from either of them. They accompanied me to the elevator anyway.

Manipulating the bundle into the tiny elevator was something else altogether. I had to reverse and change angles so many times I practically needed a back-up sound, like a truck.

Berron finally pushed the obstructing end out of the way so the doors would close.

"Let me know if you find anything else—" I said, but the doors slammed shut before either of them could respond.

Down at the street level, I hailed a cab and tossed the clothing bundle into the trunk. A short ride later, the car stopped in front of the building that housed the fashion studio where Lily spent most of her time. I paid and hopped out. Then I slung the bundle over my shoulder and climbed to the loft.

Large windows lit the studio with natural golden light, making the sketches pinned to the wall glow. Racks of clothing cast geometric shadows. And there at the design table in the middle of it stood Lily, in high-waisted bright pink slacks and a contrasting black top. Silver links made up a necklace that jingled slightly as she shifted, and a lightweight gray scarf trailed loosely over her shoulders.

She looked up and smiled. "Aunt Zelda! What are you doing here? And what is *that*?" She dodged the table and hurried forward to greet me.

"This," I said, throwing the bundle onto a nearby work table with a *thump*, "is a donation."

Lily's deft hands quickly unrolled the quilt, revealing Prospero's clothing. She lit up and reached for the closest jacket—then she stopped before touching it, and actually shied back. Hesitantly, she picked up a red silk bow tie instead. "Where did you get this?"

"A well-dressed distant acquaintance who passed on." I'd prepared that line ahead of time.

Lily rubbed her thumbs over the bow tie. "Passed on? As in, he died?" She looked concerned. Or confused. Or something. And after her strange reading on the Midsummer Night's Dream costumes, I wasn't entirely sure what Lily's gift was—but I knew she was fully capable of surprising me. "Yes," I said. "He died. Very old." I watched her. "Is there something wrong with the clothes? Should I throw them out?"

"No!" The answer came so quickly that I jumped. She seemed to have startled even herself, because she smoothed her hands over the clothes as if trying to smooth over the odd response. "No, they're beautiful items. We can alter them for people who are starting over and need formal clothes for job interviews and so on."

"Are you sure there's nothing... *wrong* with them?" I didn't know how to ask any better. I only knew that she'd picked up *something*, and I was dying to know what it was.

"They just have a—I don't know, this is going to sound silly—"

"No, please. Go on."

"They have a sort of presence about them. Like a scent that lingers."

"Is it grape soda and cinnamon? Because I sprayed some perfume right before I handled this stuff."

Lily shook her head. "Not an actual scent. More like"—she looked at me as if I would think her crazy—"more like a memory."

The topmost jacket lay on the table with its arm pointed toward me, like an accusation. I dragged my gaze away from it. "What do you mean, 'a memory?'"

Lily held the bow tie toward me.

I took it. Held it in my hands. Rubbed my thumbs over the silk, as she had. Was it my imagination, or did I feel a wisp of vampire magic? I looked at Lily. "What do you sense from these clothes?"

"You don't think I'm weird?"

"Lily," I said, "I've seen more weird than you'll *ever* be."

She took a deep breath and placed her hands on the clothes again. "Roses," she said. She closed her eyes and said nothing for several moments. "Ice."

I caught myself inhaling sharply, then released the air slowly so as not to startle Lily.

"And there's something else..." Head bowed, she ran her hands over a tweed jacket. "More like a... *feeling*."

"Yes?"

"This is *really* weird—"

"Just say it!" It came out far sharper than I meant it to.

"A... struggle? A fight," she concluded.

My stomach slowly twisted, like a snake doubling back on itself. "In the past, though, right? You said it's like a memory."

"Not this part." She opened her eyes and rubbed her arms as if noticing a sudden chill. "You think I'm crazy, don't you. That I'm imagining I'm some kind of clothing psychic."

I was caught between wanting to comfort her and needing to keep her in the dark about things that weren't mine to reveal, like her family's magic. "Lily. Listen to me. You're not crazy. I happen to know—" I stopped and chose my next words extremely carefully. "I can tell you that you are not wrong about what you sensed."

"I'm not?"

I shook my head slowly.

"I mean, the roses and the ice were kind of pretty, really. But the other feeling... I'll be honest, Aunt Zelda. It was kind of scary! Maybe I was wrong about that one?"

I slid the bow tie in my pocket and remembered that night on the ice field, embracing my enemy for the first and last time. "I don't know, kiddo. I don't know."

5

With a stop at West Side Sandwiches to check on everything, it was dark by the time I arrived home. Jester greeted me at the door with circus poodle hops and doggy kisses, and I found my mother settled on the couch with Georgiana like a shaggy electric blanket across her lap.

"You're home!" she said. "I had the most wonderful idea!"

"Oh?" My mother's wonderful ideas could range from the truly wonderful, like *let's have ice cream for dinner*, to the less wonderful, like *why don't we go get you a nice dress, you always wear those darned tank tops and shorts.*

She waved her phone at me, looking immensely pleased with herself. "I bought us tickets to a Broadway show tonight."

"Which one?"

"Does it matter? It's Broadway!" She did jazz hands.

"Guess I'll be surprised, then."

"I invited your friend Poppy"—she leaned closer like she was about to discuss someone's embarrassing illness— "but she said she didn't like to go to the theater very often."

"Yeah, she only goes to shows where she can buy out a box and sit by herself. It's not that she doesn't like company, but when you can pick up the thoughts of everyone within six feet, it's not ideal for trying to pay attention to a show."

"Poor girl," my mom said, patting Georgiana's long back. "Can we bring her something instead? Is there anything she likes to eat?"

I chuckled. "Poppy likes anything sweet. Maybe we could bring her dessert."

My mother looked satisfied, then concerned. "Will they still be open after the show? It'll be so late."

"Mom, this is New York. You can get dessert twenty-four hours a day." I picked up a rubber ball and threw it. Jester bounced after it.

"How marvelous," she mused. "I could get used to that."

An eight o'clock showtime left enough time to shower, change, make a sandwich, and hail a cab for the theater district—once I managed to get the actual name of the theater out of my mother.

"The Hudson," she said, eyes bright in the streetlights. She wore heels and a pantsuit with a statement necklace, and an overcoat borrowed from me that nearly dragged the ground thanks to our height difference.

"Oh, I know that one. Isn't that the one with the Sondheim revival?"

"That's the one. There'll be singing, and dancing, and that cute young man from those movies, and that other cute young man from that other movie..."

"Are we going to see a musical or cute young men?"

She nudged me playfully. "Why choose?"

The evening wind twirled fallen leaves as we got into the cab. Anticipation made the short ride feel like slow motion. The city came alive at night as if everything was electrified—not just the lights, but the people themselves, buzzing with energy that flung itself against the early darkness of the season.

We were dropped off on 44th Street a few steps from the theater itself. A marquee trimmed with gold overhung the sidewalk, and wood and glass double doors led into a small but ornate lobby. Green marble with gold veins covered the walls. Stern female statues in gold flanked each of the two ticket windows. Since we already had our tickets, we continued to the inner lobby.

Unlike the heavy green marble of the ticket lobby, the inner lobby glowed with an illuminated bar and mirrors set in arches along the walls. Overhead, three large stained glass domes shed a warm light on the crowd.

My mother excitedly grabbed my arm and pointed to the domes. "I read about those! They're *Tiffany*." She whipped out her phone and snapped pictures.

She was right to be impressed. You couldn't see the intricacy of the decorations and *not* be impressed. So I stood patiently until she'd filled her camera roll and then gently dragged her toward the theater when the showtime announcement rang out.

We settled in our seats, and in a few moments, the show began.

After the curtain rose, I'm not sure I followed the plot so much as I sat back and let it wash over me. Sitting next to my mom in the darkened theater made me even more aware of her presence—that she was really in New York, after all these years of avoidance, happily doing the tourist thing as if this trip had been planned on purpose. Out of the corner of my eye I could see her smile and laugh at all the right moments, as caught up in the show as anything I'd ever seen her do.

At times, I wanted to stop the show, to turn to her as the orchestra fell silent, and ask: *Why are you here?* But before she could answer, even in my imagination, the orchestra leader would strike up the music once again and the actors on stage would swing into motion like they'd never stopped.

Intermission brought another chance to meander through the lobby, and, at Mom's insistence, a chance to push through the crowd and peek into the private lounge upstairs. By the time the second act had begun, she was bouncing in her seat with excitement. I hadn't seen her so delighted in years—and that entertained me more than any amount of song and dance onstage.

When the curtain finally fell, my mother leaped to her feet and applauded enthusiastically. "Wonderful! Oh, my! It was just *wonderful*. Didn't you think so, Zelda?" she added, as we made our way outside.

"Definitely," I said. "But aren't you tired, Mom? I know you said you wanted to pick up something for Poppy, but—"

"Nonsense! I'm brimming with energy." She turned around on the sidewalk like Jester chasing his own tail pouf. "Where's the nearest bakery?"

"The one up the street is open late," I said.

"Lead on!" she cried, with a merry flourish.

We continued on foot, away from the bright lights of the theater district. Rarely were the streets of Manhattan not occupied by pedestrians and cars, even at a late hour, but the traffic had thinned until the closest people who shared the street were only vague silhouettes in the distance, and the cars slid by one or two at a time.

Drafts bolted out from between the buildings and ran down the street from east to west. I pulled my hat down and offered Mom my scarf to add to hers.

"I'm fine, Zelda girl. Don't you worry about me," she said.

I had already started formulating a plan about what to order for dessert when we reached the tiny cupcake shop. The *shop* wasn't tiny—not with its broad, shining steel counters, and generously-sized display cases—but the cupcakes were.

The flavors marched in perfect rows: miniature peanut butter and jelly cupcakes, chocolate chip pancake cupcakes, tie-dye-colored cupcakes, cookie dough cupcakes, and many more. Every kind of cupcake flavor you could imagine, all in bite-sized form. If you were going to buy a dozen, it paid to have a battle plan going in.

While my mother wrung her hands and hemmed and hawed over the many choices, I confidently rattled off eleven of the best. "Did I miss any you wanted?" I asked her.

"What about the white chocolate hot cocoa one?"

"And one white chocolate hot cocoa cupcake," I finished, to the shop clerk.

They boxed the order in a clear plastic container and slid it across the steel counter.

We took our prize and returned to the cold night, heading back to a more populated street to catch a cab. The walk was quieter than usual, the neighborhood emptied like the Hudson Theater stage after a show.

So quiet, in fact, that I heard a soft voice down down the alley we were passing.

A soft voice saying my name.

Zelda.

I stopped short. "Was that you?"

"Was *what* me?"

"You didn't say my name?"

"No, I didn't say your name."

I peered down the alley. Nothing but dripping gutters and a shattered wooden crate.

Zelda. The voice drifted like a dry leaf, scraping along the stone sides of the buildings.

"Do you hear that?"

"Hear what?"

"Someone is in that alley, and they're saying my name."

Mom clung to my arm. "Don't you even *think* about going in there. Someone will bop you on the head and steal all your money."

"All five bucks? Oh, no!"

"Don't sass your mother."

I squeezed her hand with affection as I removed it from my arm. "Hold the cupcakes. I'll be right back."

"Zelda Hawkins, don't you dare leave me here!"

I was already moving into the alley. No normal person would go into a dark alley late at night. But I wasn't normal, not by a long shot. I'd left normal behind when I first crossed the threshold of Victorine's Upper East Side mansion.

The spinning drafts of cold air increased. Discarded candy wrappers tumbled across the ground. Above me, the moon hung in the gap between buildings. Behind me, my mother's anxious silhouette.

Zelda.

"All right," I said, slowly turning to survey every bit of the alley I could see. "I've been to a Broadway show. I've had enough theatrics for one night. What do you want?"

The wind shifted. My hair danced in my face, obscuring my vision. Beyond the now-tangled locks, a blue glow appeared.

I pushed my hair back and watched the blue glow crackle through the air before me. In the center of the glow, an outline formed.

Human-shaped.

Details sketched themselves in blue light as if they had to be conjured from memory. A jacket. Trousers. A full head of hair. A neatly trimmed beard.

A hand holding a cane.

A curse slipped out before I could even think about whether my mother would be offended.

The whispery voice firmed into the buzz on an electric fence. "Zelda..."

I swallowed, finding my own voice had gone into hiding somewhere in my shoes. "Prospero." I stepped one foot back, making myself a smaller target, and I ignited silver flames in both palms. "You're dead."

His hand rose, reaching for me.

All of a sudden, a screech erupted behind me. The sound ricocheted off the walls like a silver bullet, accompanied by the clatter of high-heeled footsteps over uneven ground.

"Mom! Stay back!"

She barrelled past me, a compact whirl of bouncing hair and flapping jacket and wildly waving hands. "You leave my Zelda alone, you *monster*!"

"Mom, no!" But before I could say another word, she flung the cupcake box through the air.

It hurtled end over end, catching the moonlight before bursting open with a plasticky pop—and then, all twelve bite-sized cupcakes showered down on Prospero and exploded like icing-covered grenades.

Fire rolled up the sides of the buildings. My arms went up instinctively, covering myself as the smoke of burned sugar filled the air. Heat warmed my bones and fiery afterimages blinded me. Despite the panic that surged through me, I was already trying to feel my way forward. To find my poor mother, who had run straight into danger.

To protect *me*.

Guilt surged along with the panic. "Mom? Are you okay? Where are you?" My eyes stung from sugared smoke and tears. Finally, I stopped where I stood and scrubbed my face with Poppy's scarf.

When I looked up, a cloud of smoke veiled the moon.

In the blackness of the alley itself, I could see nothing—

Until I saw a hunched figure, heaving with breath.

The figure straightened. Coughed. And displayed tiny flames, like pilot lights, in both palms.

Another attacker? I raised my hands, ready to fight fire with fire. *Where was Mom?*

"Where'd it go?" said a very familiar voice. "Did I get it?"

"*Mom*?" I said, unable to stop looking at her lit-up hands.

"I didn't expect all that smoke," she said. "Is it always like that?"

My brain slowed to a stop like rush hour traffic.

My *mother. Fire magic.*

"Hello?" She waved a flaming hand at me. "Are you all right?"

"Fire magic," I said. "How long have you—" I paused, thoughts falling into place like ham cubes falling into a skillet. "You wouldn't hug me when you got here. You said you were *sick*. You weren't sick. You didn't want me to *know*."

"I didn't know how to tell you—"

"Like this: 'Zelda, I have fire magic.'"

"It wasn't that easy!"

"And throwing a cupcake fireball was?"

The discomfort on her face rapidly turned into annoyance. "Don't be ridiculous. You were in danger. What else was I supposed to do?"

We weren't supposed to be discussing any of this out in the open, but after your mother's hurled a frosted fireball at a blue ghost, discretion really isn't on the menu anymore. "You didn't come here for a visit," I said. "You came here because of *this*." I gestured at the scorched walls.

Mom lifted her chin. "I did come for a visit," she said. "I just had a little extra reason."

"A little extra? A little *extra*?" A laugh burst out and echoed off the stone walls. I laughed so hard it puffed out in vapor clouds in the moonlight. My mother, the witch. I should have known when she walked in the door. I should have known when she wouldn't get close to Poppy. I should have known when she *wouldn't hug me*.

We were all magical now, the line unbroken: my grandmother, my mother, my brother, me. My aunt, my cousin, her daughter. Embrace it or hide it, the magic would come for you in the end.

I closed my hands, extinguishing my own flames. My mother, watching me, did the same.

We learn fast when we learn from each other.

"Come on," I said. "We have to get out of here before someone notices your attempt to burn down New York."

"It wasn't that bad, was it?" She looked genuinely concerned.

"No, Mom." I put my arm around her and felt, for the first time, the sensation of my mother's magic: a library stamp leaving fiery traces on my bones. An imprint that said *I love you*, and *I'll protect you*. I hugged her, and it didn't matter that she'd spent my whole life acting like magic didn't exist as long as we never talked about it.

She was one of us, now.

Patty Melt, deep in the fireplace of my mind, blinked in sleepy surprise, then twitched her whiskers with satisfaction.

"Let's go get some more cupcakes," I said.

6

I woke up stiff on the couch the next morning, unable to fend off Jester when he jumped on my head and began licking my face. "All right, you maniac. Get off." I sat up. Groaned when I remembered the night before.

Ghosts. Magic. "Mothers," I said, hurling a throw pillow.

Jester ran after it.

I dragged myself into the kitchen and found the replacement box of cupcakes. Pulled the liners off two of them and shoved them in my face. Chocolate, vanilla: the foundation of a healthy breakfast.

The sound of food should have brought Georgiana galloping to the kitchen. Where was she? Had Poppy gone out early?

I looked around and found a note in Poppy's handwriting on a thick, cream-colored notecard: *Have gone to visit the Princess. Took Georgiana with me. Your mum can use my room—I'll stay over in the Fortress. Such fun!*

I flipped it over. Gold engravings of leaves bordered a personalized invitation for Poppy to attend the upcoming Late Harvest

Luncheon, hosted by the League of Women's Welfare—also known as the Ladies Who Witch.

"Huh," I said, fanning myself with the invitation before returning it to the counter. Poppy had been spending a lot of time in the Forest of Emeralds since our adventure there. I couldn't blame her. It had to be a relief to not be reading everyone's minds at all times.

Jester stared at me with begging eyes as rich brown as the chocolate cake.

"No chocolate for you, bud. Bad for the tummy. How about a liver treat?" His ears perked up like shag-carpeted satellite dishes. I retrieved a freeze-dried cube and tossed it to him in exchange for a sit and a shake. If only everything were so uncomplicated.

What had I actually seen in that dark alley?

I brushed cupcake and liver crumbs off my hands and snuck upstairs to get ready to go out, careful not to wake my mother, who wasn't used to the late hours we'd kept the night before. Back downstairs, I set out a fresh bowl of water for Jester and filled up his food toys. Then I leashed him and slipped outside, closing the door quietly.

When we returned from the morning walk, I opened the door to the townhouse to the smell of eggs, sausage, and something savory of the baked goods variety. I unclipped Jester's leash, and we made our way down the hallway past Poppy's cheerful decorations. In the kitchen, my mom stood with her back to me, stirring something in a frying pan.

Jester, faithful food hound, sat politely to the side in case particles of breakfast fell on the floor.

"Oh, good," I said. "You're up."

"Of course I'm up. Breakfast doesn't make itself." She stepped back from the stove and gestured to the pots and pans. "Cheese grits, cheese omelets"—she put on one of my silicone oven mitts and pulled a pan out of the oven—"and cheesy sausage biscuits."

"We're getting our calcium today, I see."

"Sit, sit, sit," she said, waving the oven mitt toward the little table. "I'll make you a plate."

I sat. In my family, food deserved full attention.

Jester agreed. He trotted over to the table and sat, fully alert.

My mother busily clanked plates on the counter and spooned up grits and eggs, following those up with two breakfast biscuits each.

"Mom, I don't know if I can eat all that—"

"Nonsense. You need your strength. And it's the least I can do after giving you such a fright last night."

"About that—"

"Hush, now. Let's eat."

Far be it from me to disobey the woman who birthed me, and, more importantly, just handed me a hot breakfast. I dug in, piling grits, eggs, and biscuit into every bite.

Mom wielded her knife and fork with grace and economy, followed by delicately patting her mouth. When we finished, she swept the plates away and began to clean up the rest.

"Let me get that," I said.

"I got it," she insisted, scooping leftover grits into a bowl.

I didn't bother to argue. I just pitched in, wrapping up the biscuits and scraping the pans before depositing them in the sink to soak. "We need to go see Poppy," I said, tossing a few bits of egg to Jester.

"Oh?"

"There's no need to hide your new magic from her, and she might be able to help teach you how to use it properly."

Mom shook her head and folded a dishtowel. "I don't need her to teach me—I need her to take it *away*."

"Take it away? Why would you want to do that?"

"I'm too old for this sort of thing, Zelda. I don't want to be dealing with"—she paused, then waved her hand through the air—"all this."

"You're not serious."

"I *am* serious. It's all well and good for you. You're young."

"I'm not *that* young."

"You know what I mean."

"I really don't. I mean, this is a *gift*. I didn't know that I wanted to use my magic until I actually started using it. You haven't even tried to live with it yet."

Mom looked away.

"You're here, anyway," I said. "We'll do it together." I put my arm around her. "Who knows? It might be fun!"

"That's what people say right before everything goes to hell."

"Mom!" I gave her a little shake.

"All right, all right. I'll do it, if it'll make you happy. But if I don't like it—"

"If you don't like it, we'll do whatever we can to make you comfortable again." I didn't say *get you back to normal*, because that would have made it sound like using magic was something weird or bad. Mom already thought that way, and I had no desire to reinforce it. "Come on. Let's start now."

"Already?"

"No time like the present. Isn't that what you always told me?"

"I didn't expect you to use my wise words against me."

"Payback's a mother."

"Zelda!"

I laughed. "Let's go see Poppy."

"Where is Poppy, by the way? I didn't see her or that enormous dog of hers this morning."

"She's—" How would I explain this to my mother? Pocket universes? Parallel dimensions? Magic doors?

Magic doors it was. "You know the Narnia books?"

Mom looked half offended, half like I had lost my mind. "Of course I know the Narnia books."

"Remember how the children got to Narnia?"

"I am not climbing into a wardrobe, if that's what you're suggesting."

"Not a wardrobe. More like... a garden path."

"A garden path?"

"Poppy is in another world that's adjacent to ours. A world belonging to a people called the Gentry. You can think of them as fairies, if it helps. Berron is one of them."

She patted my arm. "All this sounds like complete nonsense, so don't fret yourself about the details. Just lead on." She glanced down at Jester. "Does he come, too?"

"Jester?" I looked down at my miniature poodle.

His jaw fell open in a doggy smile, and his tongue hung out slightly off-center.

"See?" Mom said. "He wants to go."

Jester's tongue swiped over his entire face in search of egg molecules.

I rolled my eyes. "Sure he does," I said. Then again, if it gave Mom courage, Jester couldn't be *too* much trouble. "Okay. Fine. The dog can come."

My mom leaned down to Jester. "You're coming, too! You hear that, little boy?"

Jester, clueless but enthusiastic, jumped up on his hind legs and kissed her face.

There were multiple known entry points. Gramercy Park was the one we had used at first, but after all of the ways between our world and theirs had opened, the one in Riverside Park became the go-to for sheer convenience.

We would need one of the Gentry to take us through. Since Berron was the only one who spent any amount of time outside the Forest of Emeralds, that meant I needed Berron.

While Mom bustled off to finish getting ready, I texted the Prince of the Gentry. *What's up, Your Highness?* Couldn't go straight into demanding things. I mean, I *could*, but if I started low-key, I had somewhere to build to.

A few minutes later, he replied. *I'm at the Museum of Arts and Design.*

Is that the one on Columbia Circle? I wrote back.

They have this glass flamingo goblet I'm really into, he said.

I typed quickly: *Don't steal it.*

A pause. Then: *Why not?*

I sighed and put the phone down, rethinking my life in general, then picked it back up. *Because I need you.*

I didn't know you cared, he replied.

Shut up, I typed. *I need you to take me and my mom through to Poppy.*

He sent a selfie next to the flamingo goblet. A flamingo formed the stem and supported a trumpet-shaped pink glass vessel on its head. Lit from behind with pure white light, it beamed in a kitschy, cheerful way.

Lovely, I wrote.

Me, or the goblet?

I debated the flattery before I went ahead and sent it: *Both. Now can you please stop drooling over expensive breakables and meet us at Riverside Park?*

So you're actually introducing me to your mother?

I closed my eyes and took a breath, then reopened my eyes. Needs must, as Poppy would say. *Behave*, I texted.

It wasn't until ten minutes later, when I was getting ready myself, that my phone dinged again, with his response: *Where's the fun in that?*

We bundled up for the cold, including a little jacket for Jester, and headed out.

At Riverside Park, the fallen leaves had drifted to the sides of the pathways like windblown confetti after a parade. We followed the broad, paved pathway north to the 91st Street Garden.

You would think that the garden would have fallen into a restful sort of decay, fast asleep until spring—but in fact, it was so carefully managed that even deep into autumn, it was wide awake with green plants and colorful flowers.

"Oh, my goodness, elephant ears! Japanese beautyberry! And that's billygoat weed right there," she said, pointing to a fluffy, light purple flower. She rubbed her gloved hands together with delight. "Who takes care of this garden?"

"The Garden People."

"The *garden* people?"

"No, really—that's their official name. They're volunteers. They each take care of a plot." I leaned on the fence railing and searched for a plant I could identify. Mostly I just called them *that red one*, or *that green one with the funny-shaped leaves*, but with my mother around I had to try harder. "Are those... mums?" I guessed wildly.

She beamed. "Zelda! You know what a chrysanthemum is!"

"You taught me well," I replied, hoping she didn't ask me to identify a single other plant, because I couldn't. Thankfully, I was saved by Berron's approach. "Oh, good," I said as he walked up. "You aren't carrying a stolen flamingo glass."

"Who said I didn't drop it off at your place on the way?"

"You don't have a key."

"Keys, bah," Berron said, waving away the minor inconvenience of locks. "And is this your lovely mother?" he added, fixing Mom with a smile.

"Mom, this is my friend, Berron. He helped renovate the shop and make the furniture for it. Berron, this is my mom, Effie."

Mom patted her hair. "Charmed, I'm sure."

Berron draped his arm over my shoulder and gave me a side-hug that turned into something more like a side-earthquake. "Do you know what your daughter did?"

"Berron, I don't think we need to get into all that—"

He gave me another shake to shut me up. "She's so modest. If your daughter hadn't intervened, some very bad things would have happened to the people I care about. I know if she's that special, you must be something special, too."

My mother giggled. "I like this one. You can keep him."

"Mom, I'm not keeping anyone—"

"Mother knows best," Berron said, patting my shoulder before releasing me. "Now, shall we enter the garden?" He unlatched the gate and held it open.

"Don't mind if I do," Mom said. She took quick and dainty steps down the pathway.

I leaned close to Berron's ear. "Stop buttering her up."

"It's not butter if it's sincere," he murmured.

I rolled my eyes and let Jester drag me further in.

Berron looked up and down the pathway adjacent to the garden, making sure no one was in sight, before hurrying after us. "It's all clear,"he said.

The garden was laid out in a simple rectangle surrounded by a low black fence. A brick path, straight as the Manhattan grid but only wide enough for a single person, cut the space down the middle. The path led to an open space, square-shaped, like a patio. Everything growing in the garden was no taller than shoulder height, making it easy to see in and out.

"Are we supposed to disappear from here?" my mother asked. "Wouldn't that be a little suspicious to the people walking past?"

"That's what Berron was checking," I said.

Berron caught up and held out his hand to my mom. She took it, bouncing slightly in anticipation.

I took her free hand, forming a chain—Berron, Mom, me, and Jester—and looked around one last time. "We're clear. Go."

Berron continued along the path. It felt less like a path and more like a runway now, though we weren't running. The plants seemed to pass us by quicker than we were walking, blurring like an Impressionist painting in the Met. Colors merged and melted. The air sang with golden magic. Our shoes struck the brick path until suddenly they didn't, going soft and quiet over a springier surface. Only then did new surroundings rise up around us, replacing the low garden plots with towering trees, a soaring leafy canopy, and unfamiliar birdsong.

"Oh, my," Mom said, coming to a stop and gazing around with wonder and a touch of bewilderment.

"Welcome," Berron said, "to the Forest of Emeralds."

Jester immediately set about sniffing the ground like it was his job.

Mom gripped my shoulder, steadying herself. "Where are we, exactly?"

"In the Forest of Emeralds, like Berron said."

She let go and shot me a look. "I know that, Zelda, but where *are* we? Did we walk right off a map?"

Berron jumped in. "More like we're on another map, underneath a map of Manhattan. Or on top of it. I've never been quite sure about the positioning." He beckoned her forward and guided her to the top of a low rise.

Mom stood straight, listening carefully and surveying the land as Berron pointed out the relative locations of familiar tourist landmarks to their counterparts in the realm of the Gentry.

"Remarkable," Mom said. "All my life, I never imagined..." She swept her hand to indicate the landscape.

All of it green and rich, a far cry from what it had been on my first trip. If only she could have seen what it took to restore it. All of us, in our own ways, bending the magic to bring an enchanted forest back to life. I was proud of what we'd done. "Still want to get rid of your magic?" I asked.

"Of course I do," she replied quickly. "I was just remarking on how *impressive* this was."

I nodded, unwilling—for once—to argue. Magic was nothing to take lightly, I'd learned.

As beautiful as it was, if you let it into your life, it might never let you go.

7

We walked down from the grassy ridge toward the Fortress of Apples, which rose like a stone wedding cake from the great apple orchard that surrounded it. A hushed wind ruffled the leaves and made the apples sway, filling the air with the scent of fruit.

In front of the fortress, an archery target had been set up. At a distance was a wooden rack with two bows, and two quivers filled with arrows. There was no one in sight—unless you counted Sybelia the horse, who peeked around a trunk and whickered at the sight of us. Her coat shone, and the dappled galaxies on her side shifted as if the very universe was expanding and contracting with each breath.

Georgiana the wolfhound loped out from the orchard.

Having spotted his favorite horsey friend and his enormous roommate, Jester lunged at the end of the leash.

I reached down and unclipped him. He couldn't come to harm here, not in the Forest of Emeralds, where every being would look out for him. The Gentry spoiled him even more than I did.

He bolted to Sybelia and play-bowed, like he would to another dog. Sybelia danced lightly on her hooves, and Jester responded in kind, dodging left and right excitedly, with happy barks. Georgiana ran around them in circles, her shaggy tail flying.

"Whose horse is that?" my mother asked.

"That's my horse. Sybelia," Berron said.

"And is that your castle?"

Berron sketched a bow.

"Oh, my." She elbowed me sharply, probably thinking it was subtle.

"Ow!"

She gestured with her head toward the Fortress, as if I'd never noticed it before and needed to be prodded to realize there was a giant stone structure in front of us.

"Mom, what on Earth are you doing?"

She rolled her eyes.

I knew what she was doing. She wanted me to take note that here was Berron, a seemingly nice fellow—if not entirely human—and here was a castle that belonged to him, and why couldn't I put two and two together and simply lock him down without further delay.

I sighed. Between this, and Daniel being *such a nice boy*, I was tempted—again—to put my mother on an airplane.

Voices carried from the distance: Poppy's round, clear British tones, followed by the low, rich murmur of the Princess of Arrows. They emerged from around the curve of the lowest level of the Fortress of Apples, Poppy carrying a large mug that steamed.

"Zelda!" cried Poppy. "And Zelda's mum! Oh, how delightful." In her hurry to approach, whatever was in the mug sloshed over the rim and pattered on the grass.

The Princess of Arrows, more stately, did not hurry, but a warm look of welcome brightened her serene face.

"Mom, you know Poppy, of course. And this is Berron's sister, the Princess of Arrows."

"Pleased to meet you," Mom said. She leaned close to me and spoke quietly. "Do we shake hands? Do I curtsy?"

The Princess of Arrows held out a delicate hand. "I am so pleased to make your acquaintance, Mother of Zelda."

"Please, call me Effie. And do you go by... Princess?"

"I am called the Princess of Arrows."

My mother paused, as if waiting for something more. "No name?"

The Princess of Arrows looked momentarily at a loss.

Berron jumped in smoothly. "Our ruler goes by their title."

"Oh, my goodness—I've offended you," Mom said. "Look at me, putting my foot right in my mouth!"

"It is not so," the Princess of Arrows said, stepping forward and slipping her arm through my mother's. "I am not offended. Indeed, I am most pleased to welcome you to the Forest of Emeralds. May I offer you some refreshment? The Fortress of Apples has anything you might require. Do you care for sapphire-berry punch, Effie?"

"That sounds *wonderful*."

"Then you must try it. And as we walk, you must tell me of all your adventures in the city of New York."

They strolled away through the apple grove, the Princess of Arrows's golden dress trailing behind her.

"That went quite well," Poppy said.

"What, did you think my mom would freak out or something?"

"No." She took a long pull from her mug. "Yes." She eyed Berron speculatively. "Speaking of titles, what's *your* title?"

"What do you mean?" he said.

"Princess of Arrows," Poppy said, gesturing toward where my mother and the Princess had wandered off. "Prince of...?"

"I'm afraid it's just 'Prince of the Gentry.' Although I do have a tree."

"A tree?" I said.

"The Prince's Tree."

Poppy and I traded looks. "Care to elaborate?" I said.

"It's in a valley not far from here. It's an unusual tree, with a split trunk—almost like it has two legs—and a sort of a nook where you can sit against the trunk and think. I spent so much time sitting there that everyone started calling it... well, you know." He smiled.

I had to admit, it sounded *exactly* like Berron to have his very own royal tree.

"Oh, look, there's your mum!" Poppy said. "Yoo-hoo! Over here!"

My mother appeared to have completely changed her clothes. Her sensible fall outfit had been replaced by billowing bronze-colored robes that fluttered and sparkled with tiny gems. She held an enormous goblet and alternated sipping with one hand and gesturing animatedly with the other as she and the Princess of Arrows approached.

"Zelda!" my mom cried. "Have you tried this"—she leaned toward the Princess of Arrows and placed a familiar hand on her arm—"I do declare, I cannot remember the name. Bumble-berry?"

"Sapphire-berry," the Princess of Arrows said.

"Sapphire-berry!" my mother repeated, triumphantly, releasing Berron's sister's arm with a friendly pat. "Have you tried it?" she asked me again.

"No..." Her eyes certainly were sparkly. Was it the clear, almost prismatic light of the Forest of Emeralds?

She swayed gently, causing her robe to ripple like slow-breaking waves on Sparkle Beach.

Ah.

My mother was ever-so-slightly tipsy.

I shot Berron a look.

"Don't look at me," he said.

The Princess of Arrows beamed goodwill like sunshine. "It is considered most hospitable to offer guests a relaxing refreshment upon their arrival. Sapphire-berry is the traditional drink of welcome."

My mother took another sip and smacked her lips.

"I see," I said. "Berron didn't offer us any when we first got here."

"What, like I needed a drunk Daniel tearing up my room?"

"Drunk?" Mom said, straightening up with all the dignity of a tiny Southern woman. "No one's *drunk*. I am merely"—she hiccupped—"*relaxed*."

I held my hand out for the cup, intending to try it but also to get it away from her, since we had fire magic to try out and I didn't want to be flamed like a creme brulee. "May I?"

She steadied the goblet with both hands and passed it over.

I took it, eyeing each of the others in turn, not sure what I was in for. Then I touched my lips to the rim and tilted the goblet.

The scent hit me first. Something like blueberries and blackberries, with an herbal, minty edge. The juice flowed across my tongue, slightly sweet, but bubbly like champagne. Suddenly my mind filled with long-forgotten memories of golden light, puffy white clouds, and warm breezes from long-ago Florida beach vacations. Lost sensory impressions of the warmer months wrapped me in sapphire-berry-induced bliss. "Whoa," I said.

Mom reached for the goblet.

"Hang on a second." I took another sip. Sun-heated grass beneath my feet. The soothing drone of bumblebees. Sea salt in the air. I licked my lips involuntarily, almost sure I could taste the beach and wasn't just remembering it. "You've been holding out on me, you two," I said, pointing to Berron and the Princess of Arrows.

"Do you like it?" she asked.

"Like it? I wish I could bottle and sell it!" I peered into the cup and realized I'd only left a sip. My cheeks warmed. "Here, Mom. Finish it off."

"Thank you," she said, taking the cup. She tossed it back neatly. "Mm-mm. That's just lovely!"

The Princess of Arrows took the empty goblet and looked gratified. "It is one of our seasonal brews."

"There are *more* like this?" I said.

She nodded. "Oh, indeed there are. You must return to us many times, my dear friends, to sample them all."

"We should be back several times," I said. "Mom needs to practice her magic."

"Oh, yes," my mom chimed in.

I blinked at her. This was my mother, the same woman who—barely an hour ago—declared she was too old for this and should probably pass off her magic to someone else, if possible.

She gave a tiny shrug, almost sheepishly. "Why not? Especially if it involves such charming people," she said, gesturing to Berron and the Princess of Arrows. "And such *delicious* beverages."

"Fine," I said. "If the Gentry and their drinks can get you to try out your magic, I'm all for it."

"Right-o!" Poppy said. "Shall we begin?"

I looked around. "Where are the dogs? I'd kind of like to know before we start slinging fire."

Poppy cupped her hands around her mouth. "Georgiana! Yoo-hoo!"

"Jester!" I called.

Nothing.

I tried again. "Treat time!"

That got them. With an answering *woof* to guide me, I spotted them toward the top of the Fortress of Apples, standing on the green grass spiral that wound its way around the structure. They dashed around and around, pink tongues flapping in the air as they ran, all the way to the bottom.

"There they are," Poppy said. "Mummy's big fuzzy baby. Isn't that right, Georgiana?" She fed the wolfhound treats from her hand, expertly keeping the dog distracted until she clipped on the leash.

I did the same with Jester. "Now," I said. "Who wants to mind the canines?"

Jester was already investigating Berron's shoes. Berron put his hand out for the leash and I handed it over.

"I shall take Georgiana," the Princess of Arrows said.

Berron and his sister retreated to a safe distance, then sat comfortably on the grass with the dogs.

"Let's see," Poppy said. She took my mother's hands, peered at them, flipped them over, then raised them into the air at Mom's shoulder height, as if she might flap them and fly.

When Poppy let go, Mom relaxed her arms to her sides. "Well?"

"Show us your fire, then," Poppy said. "Just a little one, mind you. Don't go singeing my eyebrows."

"I'll try not to," Mom said. She turned one hand palm up and frowned slightly.

I backed up, remembering the fireball that exploded the first batch of cupcakes.

8

A silver flame appeared on my mother's palm. "Not very big," she said.

"No, no," Poppy said. "It's quite perfect. Hold out your hand so I can see it?"

Mom complied. Poppy supported Mom's hand from underneath, lifting it up and down; bringing it closer and further away; squinting at it and making thoughtful noises. "Now the other."

Mom brought her other hand up and a silver flame popped to life.

"Quick draw. Very nice," Poppy said, examining the newly flaming hand as she had examined the first one. Then she briskly folded my mother's fingers over, snuffing out the silver flames, and let her hands go. "Let's see. What have we got that we can set on fire without consequence?"

"Berron," I said.

"Zelda's antique boots," he retorted.

"Touch my boots and die," I said.

"I have a sheaf of dried lavender; would that help?" the Princess of Arrows asked.

"Wonderful," Poppy said.

The Princess of Arrows stood, deftly brushed off her golden gown, and took Georgiana with her back to the Fortress of Apples.

"In the meantime, why don't we give ourselves a bit of distance, yes? From the spectators," Poppy added.

I moved back. "I feel like we should be calling you Professor Poppy."

Poppy curtsied. "Professor Poppy, at your service."

The Princess of Arrows returned from the Fortress with a bundle of dried flowers. She approached and held them out to Poppy. "Will this be sufficient?"

"Oh, yes. Thank you, my little golden friend."

The Princess of Arrows smiled shyly and retreated.

"Now, Effie," Poppy said, pulling a few stems of dried lavender free. "I'm going to throw a bit of this in the air, and I want you to try to set it on fire."

"Isn't that dangerous?" my mother asked. "What if I accidentally set you on fire?"

"You can't. I have fire magic, too. I'm immune. Watch." Poppy lit the lavender with a touch and a small flash of silvery fire. She brandished the smoking lavender, then extended her other hand over it. A normal person would have instantly been burned. "*Et voila!*" She extinguished the lavender, whipped it away, and displayed her unburned hand. "See?"

My mother leaned forward, carefully examining Poppy's skin. "All right," she said. "If you're sure."

"Quite sure," Poppy said. "Ready?"

Mom nodded.

"Light one of your hands. Your dominant hand, please."

Mom held her right hand up and re-ignited the flame in her palm.

Poppy walked a short distance away and pulled out a larger spray of lavender. The dogs sat on their haunches as if they, too, were waiting for a show to begin. Then Poppy tossed the dried flowers in the air. "Fire!"

Mom thrust her hand skyward. Fire erupted in a stream of silver. When it hit the lavender, it flashed into orange and yellow before what was left of the lavender hit the ground, smoldering and smelling of smoke and perfume. Tiny red ashes ignited as if actual *fire* ants were crawling over the burned twigs. "Whew!" Mom said, breaking into a smile. "How was that?"

"And you say you're new to all this?" Poppy said. "Never used any magic before?"

"I can vouch for that," I said.

"Can I try with both hands?" Mom said.

Poppy and I looked at each other. This was... unexpected.

"Of course," Poppy said. She began to pull out another lavender bunch.

"How about the whole thing?" Mom asked.

Poppy looked up, her hand frozen in mid-motion. "The whole thing?"

"Yes, just chuck the whole thing. I bet I can get it."

"*Get* it?" Poppy said.

"You know." My mom gestured with both hands, like a magician. "Poof!"

"Poof," Poppy repeated. She looked at me.

I shrugged. "Let her 'poof' if she wants to."

"Go, Effie!" Berron called from the sidelines.

Mom steadied herself on her feet and raised both hands, palms forward.

Poppy gripped the remaining bundle of lavender and began to swing it back and forth, building up momentum. "Hup!" She tossed the bundle up and away.

The bundle hit the top of its arc, and Mom let fly. Even from many feet away I could feel the heat as twin fire blasts smoked the bundle in mid-air, causing it to explode in a fragrant cloud of ash. Cinders drifted down.

Both dogs leaned forward, their noses twitching.

Mom straightened up, breathing a little harder but radiant with triumph.

"Hurrah!" cried the Princess of Arrows, clapping her hands. "It is most exciting, is it not, brother?"

Berron was watching me. "Very exciting," he said. "Isn't it, Zelda?"

"Mm," I said. Truthfully, it was like watching Mom take up NASCAR driving. Even if she was surprisingly good at it, I couldn't help bracing for a crash. "Mom, why don't you take a break? I don't want you to hurt yourself."

"Nonsense, Zelda, I'm as fit as a fiddle. And I didn't slow you down when you decided to gallivant up here and get involved in magic, did I?"

I opened my mouth to answer, but she kept going.

"No, I did not. I said to myself, 'Effie, children are going to do what children are going to do'—"

"I was forty-five."

"Don't interrupt your mother. And I let you go—

"*Let* me go?"

"And I let you go knowing full well you could fall right on your face—"

"Thanks."

"*Because*," she continued, "I didn't want to hold you back from your dreams."

Even the dogs looked impressed. And then everyone was looking at me.

"I'm not trying to hold you back from your dreams. Until right this second, I didn't know your dreams involved hurling fireballs at dried flowers in the Forest of Emeralds."

"How would they, if I never knew those things existed? Except for the dried lavender, of course." She turned toward the Princess of Arrows. "Can I replace that for you, by the way? I was so excited I didn't even think twice about setting your lovely flowers on fire. Did it come from a shop around here?"

"I picked them myself."

"Oh." Mom paused, appearing to try to work out how, exactly, to replace the hand-picked flowers.

The Princess of Arrows regarded her with a look of politeness that seemed as if it could outlast the sun.

"Well," Mom finished, "I'm sure there's a craft store around here somewhere."

"Oh, yes," Poppy said. "There's a Michael's on 6th Avenue."

The Princes of Arrows cocked her head. "You do not wish to visit the Vale of Amethysts?"

"Visit the what of what now?" Mom said.

"Vale of Amethysts," Berron said. "A natural feature in the Forest of Emeralds."

Mom looked at me for help. I shrugged, having no more idea of what or where that was than she did.

"Is it... is it very far?" Mom said.

Berron shook his head. "A short walk over mostly level ground, at least until you reach the downward slope into the Vale itself."

The Princess of Arrows stood and brushed off her golden dress. "Shall I take you now?"

"Now?" Poppy said.

"Have you aught to do elsewhere?"

"Sister," Berron said, gently, "they may have obligations."

She lowered her head and folded her hands. "My enthusiasm is too great," she said. "To have such visitors quite overwhelms me."

My mother hurried forward and placed her arm around the wilting Princess. "Don't you fret. Of course we'd love to see the Vale of Amethysts, wouldn't we?" Mom looked at Poppy and me and raised her eyebrows.

"Of course," Poppy said.

"Actually, I have to get back to the shop in a little bit," I said. Time passed strangely in the Forest of Emeralds. It was easy to lose track of how long you'd been there, and get to Manhattan just as the sun was setting, having lost an entire day.

Berron stood. "I'll go with them." Jester tugged at the leash, eager to go anywhere and do anything.

"I wasn't saying there needed to be a dude to keep them safe."

"Neither was I," Berron replied easily. "My sister could outfight me blindfolded."

"This is true," the Princess of Arrows said.

I remembered Berron throwing a chair across the restaurant, and wondered what a sibling battle might look like, and how the delicate-looking Princess could overpower Berron's height, strength, and grace.

I really had to stop admiring him.

"Before you go," Berron said, approaching me and drawing me away, toward the trees. They closed around us like velvet curtains, though we were only steps away from Poppy, Georgiana, my mother, and the Princess of Arrows. He scooped up Jester in his arms and smoothed his floppy, fuzzy ears. "Don't mistake me," he said. "I didn't volunteer to go because they need a chaperone. I volunteered because your mother is going."

"My mother? What's she got to do with it?"

"You protected my family. I will protect yours."

"What harm could come to her here?"

"That's not the point. It is my obligation." With that, he suddenly sounded more formal—a hint of what he might have sounded like all the time if he hadn't spent so much time in New York.

"It doesn't have to be your obligation."

"Why are you so stubborn? Why do you get stuck on little words like 'obligation'? I won't argue with whatever I am to you, Zelda. Just let me pay you back in this way."

The quiet wood was a church, making his words sacred. Even Jester had gone serious, looking at me with brown eyes that were large and solemn.

It was easier to meet the dog's gaze than Berron's. So I gave Jester gentle scritchy-scratchies under his chin as he rested contentedly in Berron's arms.

Berron held the dog up to my face, where I was promptly licked. "See? He thinks it's a good idea."

"Jester thinks biting electrical cords is a good idea." Could I keep avoiding eye contact with Berron, maybe forever? It didn't seem likely.

"Jester isn't afraid to have someone else take care of things."

I laughed. "He's a dog, Berron. Of course he isn't. Come on, let's get back before everyone thinks we're making out in the woods."

"'*Making out*'?" Berron made a face like he'd bitten into a very garlicky pickle. "I don't 'make out.'"

"You should try it sometime," I said—and instantly regretted it, because it sounded like an invitation. Why did my appetite always betray my common sense?

"Never," he answered, placing Jester on the ground and letting him lead us back into the open grass. "I will never do anything that can be described in such low terms."

9

I opened the door and welcomed the blast of warm, bread-scented air. West Side Sandwiches was home. Even when everything was wrong, this place was right. My mind full of lunch ideas, I didn't quite register who was standing behind the counter, wearing a white apron, slowly and carefully attempting to cut a tomato.

Daniel, my ex-boyfriend, Lord of the Blessed. Being taught how to slice a tomato.

By Jessica.

With *my* knife.

Flames boiled in my palms before I had enough control to snuff them out.

James popped up from behind the glass case. "Hey, what are you doing here?" he said. "Aren't you supposed to have some time off today?"

"Who got my knife out?"

James, sensing my mood, began to inch sideways, possibly to avoid being killed when I finally decided what I wanted to throw at

Jessica and Daniel. "Oh, uh—your knife? I didn't have anything to do with that. I was just refilling this case here..."

I walked on without hearing the rest, and invaded the tight galley space.

Daniel looked up. "Hey, Zelda! Jessica was just teaching me how to cut a tomato the right way." He stepped back from the cutting board and lifted the knife, as if I didn't see it already.

Entwined magic sparked up and down the blade. My skin pricked as if there were an electrical connection. "Really. *Jessica* was teaching you."

Jessica forced a brazen smile.

"With *my* knife."

Her smile faltered.

Daniel, not exactly fast on the uptake but not stupid, either, laid the knife on the cutting board and wiped his hands on his apron. "She said you'd been teaching her. You know I'm no good in the kitchen, so I asked her to show me."

I loomed closer to Jessica until she was practically scooting up onto the counter. "I'd like to see that."

Daniel slid the cutting board over.

"Not that knife," I said, moving back a fraction of an inch so Jessica could reach for one of the regular knives.

She turned around to face the cutting board, her short hair falling forward and obscuring her face, and began to slice.

"Wrong," I said, moving in from the side and rearranging her grip on both the tomato and the knife. I braced her knife hand and moved the blade the proper way, feeling some of her Blessed power begin to move into my fingers.

I'll admit: I was angry.

So I didn't just let it sting and spiral its way up my arms. I let her thorny red vampire magic set its hooks—and then I *pulled*, not passively receiving but actively drawing the power away.

Jessica gasped. "What are you—"

I kept my grip and finished, leaving a perfectly cut tomato slice behind. "Don't. Touch. My knife," I said. I picked up my special blade and tenderly wiped the steel with a clean side towel.

Jessica patted herself down as if she'd lost her keys. "What did you do to me?"

"I reminded you who's in charge."

Fury lit her eyes. "You're not in charge of me."

I carefully replaced my knife in its case. "Is that so? Who's in charge of you, then?"

Her gaze flicked uncertainly to Daniel. "*He* is the Lord of the Blessed."

I closed the case and latched it. Then I looked at Jessica. "And who turned the Lord of the Blessed?"

She looked down at the floor and mumbled something.

"I'm sorry, I didn't catch that."

Daniel opened his mouth as if to say something, but I held up a finger.

"You did," Jessica said.

"Then if he's not doing his job... I will. Capisce?"

She nodded.

"Take five." I turned my back on her and returned the case to its cabinet. When I turned around again, Jessica was gone, the front door was swinging shut, and Daniel was staring at me.

"Little harsh, don't you think?"

"Take that apron off, I can't hear you when you look ridiculous."

He pulled it off and tossed it on the counter. "I saw what you did to her."

"So?"

"You didn't need to do that."

"Oh, no? If you don't show their kind who's boss, they'll walk all over you."

"There is no 'they' anymore. I'm '*they*.'"

"No, you're not—"

"And so are you. You said it yourself: who turned the Lord of the Blessed?"

I looked away.

"Answer me."

"I did." I leaned on the counter, my hands flat on the cold metal, letting my head fall forward. "I did," I repeated. Oh, how I promised myself I wouldn't get caught up in magical drama.

And here I was, power-tripping over a tomato slice.

I was a fool.

"I'm a fool," I said.

"Yes, you are."

A bitter laugh escaped my lips. "Thanks a lot."

A warm hand touched my shoulder. "You're a fool because you try to be responsible for everything. For Jessica. For the Gentry. For me. Your mother's probably throwing you for a loop right now, too, isn't she?"

I straightened up. "How did you know?"

He tilted his head and gave me a look.

"Okay, yeah. You're right. Maybe it's all a bit much."

He gave my shoulder a friendly pat and stepped back. "See? I'm right."

"Rarely," I said, but I was too busy trying to process what had just happened. Daniel didn't pass up chances to raise the heat level to something interesting, even if it was just to pass the time. He had moves as smooth as turning up the gas on the range. Yet he had patted my shoulder like a priest and moved further away.

Honestly—I wasn't offended so much as I felt like we'd started a new dance, one for which I didn't know the steps.

"Jessica's not so bad, anyway," he added.

"Oh?"

He shrugged.

Suddenly the steps were becoming clearer, like an old-fashioned dance diagram with arrows and footprints. "How's that going, anyway? Living with Jessica."

"She's not a terrible roommate."

"She teaches you how to slice tomatoes and everything, huh?"

"What are you implying, Zelda?"

"What are you doing, Daniel?"

"Is it any of your business?"

"No." I smiled and crossed my arms. "But I love being nosy."

"Stay out of it."

I didn't need to be a vampire to scent blood. "Not on your life," I said. "You're sweet on her, aren't you?"

He rubbed his hands over his head. "Oh, my God. Don't start."

"Is that the wrong word, 'sweet'? 'Seduce' sounds vulgar. Or are you letting her think she's doing the seducing? That would be more like you."

"Am I not allowed to be attracted to someone? Is that what this is?"

"Of course you're allowed to be attracted to someone. I just think we ought to look at *why*."

"*We* don't need to do anything."

"You can't stand it, can you? That she has one over on you."

Daniel scoffed. "What is that supposed to mean?"

"She overpowered you. It kills you, doesn't it?"

"Spare me the armchair psychology."

"Then look me in the eye and tell me I'm wrong."

He looked me in the eye. His eyes glinted red, as usual, but this time they reminded me of dark stars, glowing deeply in the night sky, distant and alien. He said nothing.

"Don't do this to hurt her," I said.

"I'm not."

"Don't do this to win."

"I think it'll be a draw," he said.

It was the only thing he could have said that would have made me believe him. She scared him. And how did Daniel deal with fear and awe? He captured the source of it, like a butterfly collector.

I had been a butterfly, once. I even enjoyed it. But now...

I was free. Just as my power over him had ended, so had his over me. I searched for regret but found only a new freedom, like rising bread, in the place where sadness should be. *Daniel and Jessica.* Stranger things had happened.

I chuckled.

"What?" Daniel said.

"I get you."

"Are you coming up with another way to insult me?"

I shook my head.

"You're smiling."

"Am I?"

"Does that mean you're going to plant that knife in my spine when I turn around?"

"No." I clapped his shoulder, then gripped it. "Unless you mess with Jessica. Then I can't promise anything." I gave him a little shake and let him go.

"Why are you so concerned that my intentions are good? You hate Jessica."

"Your intentions are twisted, just like she is. If you don't screw it up, you'll be perfect for each other."

"They're never going to put that on a Valentine card."

"They should. There should be a whole lineup: *Valentine's Cards for the Twisted, Messy, and Complicated.*"

We looked at each other, both of us knowing that we had been all of those things together.

But maybe we could be something new, apart.

James, who had been keeping quiet and out of the way, piped up. "Yeah, there's nothing that can go wrong with a crush on Jessica. I should know."

"Thank you for the input, James," Daniel said.

James waved. "Anytime." He turned and looked out the window. "Table for"—he counted by pointing—"one, two, three... do dogs count?"

"Yes," I said.

"Five, then. Table for five."

Shadows flicked across the floor as a bustling group passed in front of the windows. Two tall silhouettes, one short. Then the door opened to the shuffle and huff of Jester and Georgiana leading the way, followed by Berron, Poppy, and my mother.

A fuzzy black blur cannonballed into me.

"Jester!" I cried, scooping him up. "Did you keep everyone safe on their big trip? Did you guard them from fierce monsters with your buffness?"

"He is a hero to all," Berron intoned solemnly.

"Of course you were," I said, kissing Jester's wooly head and running my hand over his silky ears.

"I can take none of the credit," Berron added.

"I wasn't giving you any."

Berron noticed Daniel behind the counter. "Daniel," he said.

"Berron," Daniel replied.

"James," Poppy said, holding out Georgiana's leash, "could you hold her for a moment so I can get some coffee?"

"I'll get the coffee," Daniel said.

"Slicing tomatoes *and* serving coffee? We'll make a restauranteur of you yet," I said.

"Yes, I've always had a secret dream of leaving my high-paying job to serve sandwiches."

"You had him slicing tomatoes?" Berron asked.

"*Jessica* had him slicing tomatoes," I said, raising one eyebrow and giving him a *can-you-believe-it* look.

"Fascinating," Berron murmured, although his gaze lingered on me rather than shifting to Daniel.

The door swung open again, admitting the vampire in question. She froze in her tracks, taking in the crowd, then put her head down and speed-walked to the back room.

I followed.

She had pulled out a clipboard and was already checking produce bins when I stepped into the small space and closed the door. "Are you here to suck away the rest of my powers?" she said, concentrating on a very uninteresting bin of russet potatoes. "Or did you get enough earlier?"

"Jessica, I'm sorry. I shouldn't have done that."

Her pen tap-tap-tapped on the clipboard.

"I'm not going to insult you by saying 'I don't know what came over me,'" I said.

"You don't need to tell me what came over you. I know how you feel about Daniel."

"You do?" I said, surprised. Expecting her to wax on about jealousy, or something.

"You don't want him."

"I don't?" Jessica was wrong-footing me left and right.

She gave me a look. "Don't be stupid. Of course you don't. You like his attention, right? It's like the heat of the sun. Nice at a distance. Not the kind of thing you want right up in your face all the time. You'd melt."

"And you won't?"

She met my gaze without blinking. "I eat stars for breakfast."

I stared at her. It's not every day you share closet space with potatoes, onions, and a vampire woman who's low-key threatening to annihilate or possibly marry your ex-boyfriend. "Well, then," I said, at a loss for words. "I guess that's all hunky-dory. I'll let you... get back to it," I finished, gesturing to the bins. I opened the door and was almost about to leave when suddenly a thought occurred. "So, just asking—no reason—if the Lord of the Blessed were to take a consort, would that person become... a Lady of the Blessed?"

"Funny," Jessica said, almost absently, "I never thought of that."

"I'm sure you didn't," I said, slipping out and shutting the door. I had to stop and lean on it for a second.

Truthfully? They would be perfect for each other.

10

Although I hadn't originally planned on attending the Late Harvest Luncheon, my mother's arrival spurred Poppy into a frenzy of wrangling two more invitations. Poppy thought she was being discreet when she stepped into another room to have that conversation, but I overheard half of it.

"What do you mean, Zelda can't come because she's not a full member?"

Silence.

"Don't say she's not a real witch, that's *rude*—"

More silence.

"I'm not saying you have to make her a full member, just let her come to tea—" Poppy's footsteps thumped back and forth as she paced, followed by Georgiana's four-footed echo. "Right," she interrupted whoever had been speaking. "Zelda fixed your ruddy Mirror, didn't she?" A pause. "Whether it got smashed afterward is entirely irrelevant. Do I need to talk to Azure? Because I *will* talk to Azure—"

I smiled to myself. A threatening Poppy was like a gentle wave that slowly buried you in sand until only your eyes were showing.

"Thank you," Poppy finally said. "And her mother would like to come too..."

Her opponent probably wondered what to do to make it all stop. I could have told them: *just say yes to everything*.

And that's how the three of us came to be at the Late Harvest Luncheon.

A fire so hot you could feel it across the room filled the oversized marble fireplace. Urns filled with spectacular fall flower bouquets stood on banquet tables covered with rust-red velvet cloths. Leaf garlands spiraled around the grand staircase banisters, leading to arches made of sheaves of grain. A cider fountain bubbled and frothed, surrounded by mugs shaped like apples.

My mother clapped her hands with delight. "And you said they were happy to have us come?"

"Oh, yes," Poppy said. "Absolutely thrilled."

I caught Poppy's eye.

She shrugged, what-can-you-do style, then turned her attention to the cider fountain. "How lovely! I'm quite thirsty. Zelda? Effie?"

"I'm more interested in these sandwiches," Mom said. "So *elegant*. Don't you think so, Zelda?"

"Hmm..." I said, looking over the offerings. "Beef and mustard and pickle; chicken and some kind of chutney; the classic cucumber, dill, and cream cheese; and egg and watercress. Nice," I admitted. "But do they taste good?"

"Only one way to find out," Poppy said, scooping several onto a china plate.

"Don't you want to leave room on your plate for dessert?" my mom asked.

"That's what a second plate is for," Poppy replied, continuing to stack the little sandwiches.

"They bring all this in from a very fancy place on Fifth Avenue," I said. "Probably costs, oh, a hundred dollars a head. Give or take."

"A hundred dollars?" Mom squeaked.

"Poppy's membership dues at work," I said.

"Eat up!" added Poppy, cheerfully.

Mom grabbed a plate and went for the desserts. First she chose candy robin's eggs nestled in a shredded pastry nest, then several madeleines and a miniature parfait with bright red fruit puree, and finally some chocolate petits fours decorated with icing leaves in fall colors. "I'll come back for sandwiches," she said.

"Double the desserts and I'll get sandwiches for both of us," I said.

"Deal," she said, sneaking one of the robin's egg confections into her mouth.

We carried our goodies to a nearby table. The other Ladies Who Witch glanced at us curiously but mostly seemed content to load up on treats and gossip.

As we made wreckage of the fancy food, the exterior doors were closed and the curtains drawn. Several witches wearing sparkling autumn-colored robes began to make their way through the crowd, performing small acts of elemental magic. One juggled colorful maple leaves with air streams alone. Another rotated a miniature planetary system of water globes through the air while a fire witch created seasonal constellations from small pops of flame. The fourth witch carried a cornucopia of apples. The apples blushed, then rotted, then burst into tiny apple saplings from the remaining seeds, bearing small apple blossoms amid green leaves.

Everyone smiled and clapped, including my mother. "Did you see that?" she said, slapping me lightly on the arm.

I was about to reply when I heard another voice. A voice, seemingly coming from far away, deep and vibrational as if it traveled through the marble floor beneath my feet and up the bones of my legs, directly into my ribcage. Squeezing my heart instead of assaulting my ears.

Zelda.

I stopped breathing.

"Zelda?" Mom said. "Don't you like it?"

I puppeteered my head up and down. Then I made my lips do that thing where they curve upward. "Excuse me for a minute. I'll be right back."

"Do you want me to come with you, honey?"

"I'm fine," I said, quickly patting her on the shoulder before near-jogging to the hallway.

Where was it?

I looked left, then right. Upward, at the ceiling, with its elaborate crown moldings.

Zelda.

Again it vibrated up through my feet.

I looked down at the floor, which was covered by richly patterned carpet. What lay beneath the ground floor? Poppy had once taken me down a curving staircase to an art-filled chamber containing a magical dancing statue. I hurried in that direction, almost skidding on the landing before gripping the staircase railing and running down, the room twisting around me as I descended. I took the last two steps with a two-footed jump, then stumbled to the center of the room.

Colorful portraits of witches stretched the height of the room. The dancing statue, on its high, isolated perch, stood still.

"Where are you, you ghostly bastard?" I said.

Silence. Or almost silence—somewhere in the distance, water plinked like an antique piano. I hurried to a door on the other side of the room and pulled it open.

Another hallway. Unlike the hallways on the ground floor, this below-street-level hallway was dim. Stone-colored.

I stepped inside. No, not stone-colored. Actual stone. I touched the wall and condensation cooled my fingertips. "This is where you go back for help, Zelda," I said. My voice shivered back to me, a distorted echo.

I followed the hallway straight ahead to a blind right turn. I made the turn without slowing down—and had to stop on a dime, because I was three steps away from walking straight into a swimming pool.

Golden light wavered through the water, illuminating a cave-like room with an arched stone ceiling. Geometric mosaics covered the walls and the ceiling in abstract patterns; the plink-plink I'd heard came from a shell-like fountain set in the far wall above the pool.

"I heard you," I said, feeling like an idiot for talking to the empty air but pushing on. "I *felt* you. Where are you?"

Plink. Plink. Plink. Seconds dripped by.

"Don't call my name if you don't want me to show up!"

A disturbance shimmered the water, causing the light bouncing off it to shatter like pieces of a mirror. Tiny waterspouts spun across the pool, extending narrow tentacles upward as if they were looking for something to touch. The watery funnels threw off moisture that struck the stone floor with a sound like fat raindrops.

But not all the moisture struck the floor. Some of it levitated upward, centralizing, taking form.

Blue light.

A cane.

Clothing as stylish as it was ghostly.

"Prospero," I said.

The figure that was Prospero lost shape and reformed, shedding droplets and gathering them back into itself. I had a strange urge to adjust the reception on a TV antenna, although this was no broadcast and TV antennas hadn't existed for decades.

Zelda. This time I saw his mouth move even as the word vibrated my shin bones.

"Yes, we all know my name." I sounded brave, at least, even as the cold, damp air crawled through the gaps in my clothes. "What do you want?"

Zelda... My name dragged out like a heavy weight on a chain.

Cold, so much cold. My bones hurt. I didn't want to be here. I wanted to be upstairs, warm and laughing with Mom and Poppy, clinking mugs of cider. No more regrets. No more ghosts. Maybe I couldn't have normal, but couldn't I—for once—have *peace*?

He was falling apart. His hands were going first; I could see clearly because he was reaching toward me like he had in the alley.

"What do you *want*?" I cried.

A pause. A sound like static as his eerie blue glow shuddered and cracked.

Beware!

And with that one word, the figure of Prospero blew apart, throwing water in every direction.

My mouth, I realized too late, had been open.

I spat Prospero-droplets on the stone deck. I'd been so thoroughly soaked I didn't even have a dry patch of clothing to wipe my mouth on.

I wasn't scared anymore. I was *mad*. Mad that Prospero still thought he could reach out and torment me. Wasn't he supposed to be *dead*? Wasn't that how it *worked*?

And, for a moment, rage kept me warm.

But the cold crept back in, unstoppable as remembering why he was dead in the first place.

Do you think you could have made a better choice? Berron had said.

"I don't know," I said, to which only the fountain replied, with drips like tears. I turned away and squelched out of the pool cave, down the hallway, up the stairs, and back into the Late Harvest Luncheon.

Where I ran smack into Azure Washington, Witch Presiding, and her mad-eyed owl, Aloysius.

"Zelda!" Azure said. "You're all wet!"

"Oh, this?" I said, looking down at myself. "It's nothing." I tried to brush past her, but you don't brush past Azure Washington. Not if she doesn't want you to.

She put a hand out, freezing me in place without a single glimmer of magic. She gave me a onceover. Her owl did the same, its golden eyes rolling. "Do you want to explain what you've been up to?"

"I fell in the pool."

"In the pool." The way she echoed me dripped with doubt like I dripped water.

"Yes, I... was admiring it, and I leaned over too far, and, well..." I trailed off with a helpless shrug and what I hoped was a goofy grin.

"Uh-*huh*," she said. "And what exactly were you doing down there?"

"Doing?"

Her eyebrows went up another level, like side-by-side elevators. Aloysius reared back in alarm.

"I was..." Suddenly the fire witch with the tiny levitating fire stars came into view. "Hot! I was hot." I fanned myself. "It's the change, you know. All hot flash-y and sweaty." I plucked at my soaked shirtfront, realizing I might have been overdoing it.

Azure blinked in tandem with the owl. "Well. Well, then. I'm glad you were able to... cool off"—she waved her hand around—"or whatever."

"Thanks," I said, moving past as quickly as I could without seeming outright rude.

"Oh, and Zelda?" Azure said. The owl clacked its beak like punctuation.

I froze.

"Falling in the pool doesn't usually leave your back dry."

I winced but didn't dare turn around. Instead, I hoofed it over to our table.

"Where have you *been*?" Mom said. "I was about to send out a search party."

"I ran into an old acquaintance."

Poppy looked up from what appeared to be her third plate. "An old acquaintance? I wouldn't have thought you knew anyone here apart from me. And Azure and Malkin, of course."

I shifted in my seat and leaned over to examine the tea sandwiches on Poppy's plate. "Are those good? They look good."

"They are quite, quite yummy," Poppy said, brandishing one happily. "At first I thought I liked the chicken curry and mango chutney one, but then the smoked salmon one snuck up on me and—" She put the sandwich down. "Hello, are you trying to change the subject?"

"I'm just hungry." I swiped one off her plate and crammed it in my mouth, removing the possibility of talking.

"She is definitely changing the subject," Mom said. "She's no better at lying now than when she was a teenager, sneaking out of school to go someplace exotic to eat."

I swallowed. "It wasn't exotic, Mom. It was a chain teppanyaki restaurant."

My mother leaned close and lowered her voice. "What happened? You're soaking wet and you look like you've seen a ghost."

Leave it to Mom to nail it in one. "I'll tell you everything," I said. "Just let me eat all this nice, expensive food first."

"You act like it's your last meal," my mother joked, possibly to cover the fact that she looked worried.

"It's not my last meal. I promise," I said. "But I have a feeling I'm going to need my strength."

11

The demolished pastries, cookie crumbs, and jam turned the plates into an art installation that wouldn't have been out of place at the Museum of Modern Art. "Come on," I said. "I want to show you something."

"Ooh, an adventure!" Poppy said.

"Try to look nonchalant," I added.

"Nonchalant," Poppy repeated, with a broad wink that would have looked highly suspicious to anyone in a twenty-foot radius.

We eased our way through the crowd and into the hallway. I led them down the spiral stairs to the room with tall murals, columns, and the bronze dancer in its high-up niche. "Do you know what's through there?" I asked Poppy, pointing to the door across the room.

"It's a pool," Poppy said. "The water witches use it for practice. Or for swimming, too. It's really quite nice, especially if you warm it with fire magic first."

We continued through the door and into the stone hallway.

"Chilly," Mom remarked, rubbing her arms.

We turned the corner at the end of the hallway and entered the pool room with its arched ceilings and swirling geometric tile mosaics.

"Somehow I just never pictured swimming pools in New York," Mom said. "Especially not ones that looked like this."

"I guess they are pretty few and far between," I said. "Mostly in private buildings or health clubs."

"You ran into an old acquaintance *here*? Were they swimming?" Poppy said.

"Not exactly. He was floating above the pool."

"Above it?" Poppy said. "And 'he'?"

"Prospero."

They looked at each other, then me.

"*Prospero*?" Poppy said. "In the League of Women's Welfare?"

I nodded.

Poppy looked baffled. "Why would he show up at a swimming pool?"

"I don't know," I said.

Mom crouched by the pool and trailed her fingers through the clear water. "Did he manage to say anything other than your name this time?"

"Does '*Beware!*' count?"

"Well, that certainly sounds threatening," Poppy said.

All three of us fell silent, seconds still falling away with every drip of water from the shell-shaped fountain.

"Maybe he wants revenge," Poppy continued. "You *were* the enemy."

All I heard was: *You killed him.* Guilt stung like salt in a knife cut. I stared into the water until my vision blurred into dancing blue fireworks. "Poppy," I said, "can a witch banish a ghost?"

Poppy paused, appearing to think it over. "Now that's an interesting question. We witches have *elemental* magic, you see. Fire, air, water, and earth are not usually linked with ghosts and what have you. Although you do get into a bit of a gray area when you start looking at the 'soft' skills, so to speak, that are associated with each element. Like mind-reading and fire magic, for example. But it's a moot point, though, because you can't banish something that isn't here. You'd have to summon him, first."

"Summon the vampire who trashed my restaurant and nearly murdered all the Gentry?"

Poppy's hands flew to her mouth. She lowered them and whispered: "You said the v-word."

"Does it matter?" I said, the volume rising with my temper. "Really? What are all these rules we follow? Who thought them up? Who decided this particular arrangement of everything magical was the way things had to be? *Because I don't think it's working very well.*"

The last word bounced around the room, and then someone cleared their throat. Someone who wasn't me, or my mother, or Poppy.

Malkin, Azure's young witch assistant, stood framed by the archway leading into the hallway. In her tan gentleman's suit with a matching vest, a golden watch chain peeking out with a metallic glint, and short but stylish hair, she looked like a European prince—the confident gleam in her eye only emphasizing the easy way she leaned against the arch, casually demonstrating that she now controlled the only way out. "Seems like the real party's down here."

Poppy let out a panicked laugh. "We were just..." She looked at my mom and me and widened her eyes.

All I could think of was glowing blue ghosts and how I might have eaten three or four more desserts than I was supposed to.

"We were seeing if I had any latent water magic." Mom, coming through with a majestic lie. I never knew she had it in her.

Malkin strolled forward, hands in her pockets. "Oh? Have you shown any signs?"

My mother smiled charmingly. "Just fire so far. But I was hoping maybe it might show up if I tried."

Malkin shrugged off her suit jacket and held it out to me, not even pausing to see if I'd take it.

I took it.

She began rolling up her sleeves. "Why don't we do a few tests?"

"Oh!" Mom said, trying to look pleased while also looking at me and Poppy for help. "That would be wonderful!"

"Excellent," Malkin said, rubbing her hands together. "Let's start with something easy." She held one hand palm-out toward the fountain on the far wall. "See if you can catch one of those drops coming out of the fountain."

"I'll try," Mom said, slowly raising her hand to the same position.

Malkin's elemental water magic flashed like tiny silver meteors in a night sky, freezing one droplet after another.

Mom pulled her hand back and pushed it forward, as if mashing a button mounted on an invisible wall. Unsurprisingly, nothing happened. Mom's talent seemed to lie in burning things up. She lowered her arms and shrugged. "I guess it just isn't me."

Malkin released the suspended droplets and they fell into the pool.

Perhaps she would lose interest and go away.

"Let's try water that's stationary," she said.

I squeezed my eyes shut, briefly, and tried to take a silent, calming breath.

She held her hand palm-down over the pool and made a scooping motion. A cup's worth of water lifted out of the pool as if in an invisible scoop, and hovered about a foot above the pool's surface.

Then Malkin frowned.

Don't frown, I thought. *Don't notice anything unusual.*

"You said you didn't have any water magic?" she said.

Mom shook her head.

The ball of water continued to hover. Malkin looked at Poppy. "And you don't have any water magic." Her gaze shifted to me. "Have you borrowed any water magic lately?"

"Me?" Truth and lies fought a lightning battle. Which one would stop her from asking more questions? Which would be easier to defend? "No," I said.

"Funny," Malkin said, tilting her hand and making the water roll over like one of Jester's rubber balls. "There's a magic signature in the water I've never seen before. And I know all the water witches in the LWW." She released the water and let it fall.

The sudden splash made Poppy jump.

"Azure will want to know about this," Malkin said.

"Will she?" Poppy asked. "Surely it's nothing worth bothering her with."

Malkin snorted. "If there was an unknown witch's signature in your house, would it bother you?"

There was no way out but the truth. I was never going to get invited to a tea party again. "You have a ghost," I blurted.

Plink. Plink. Plink.

Damn those water droplets. They were starting to get to me.

"A ghost," Malkin repeated. "In our swimming pool."

When you're in, you're all in. "Can you take us to Azure, please? I don't want to have to explain all this more than once." I shook out her jacket and respectfully held it up, ready to be slipped into.

Malkin tilted her head, and a thick lock of hair fell over one eye as she considered. Then she stepped forward, turned around, and shrugged on the jacket like I had always been her butler. "Want to dry off first?"

"I suppose I don't need to bring the water with me," I said.

"Actually," Poppy said, "that's not a bad idea. We can use it as a sample."

"Easy enough," Malkin replied, facing me and focusing her magic. Vapor swirled away from my clothes and coalesced between her hands in a clear blob of water.

"Do you want something to put it in?" my mom asked.

"I can carry it," Malkin said.

"What about the statue?" Poppy asked. "That will set it off."

"One second," Mom said, reaching into her purse. She turned her body so Malkin couldn't see that she was emptying one of the cider cups of the extra desserts she'd stashed. She blew the crumbs out. "Here you go," she said, offering the cup to Malkin.

Malkin took it and channeled the water inside.

All magic in the off position, we followed her back upstairs.

"Is your life always this hectic?" Mom asked me.

"You don't know the half of it," I said.

We re-entered the red ballroom where the tea had taken place and followed Malkin through the side door that led to the Grand Library.

When Mom stepped inside, she stopped and placed a hand over her heart. "Oh, my stars and garters," she said. "Look at this place!" Her gaze swept the burnished dark wood floor and matching bookshelves, the intricate Persian rug, the cozy wingback chairs and the huge floor-standing globe. She went to the nearest shelves and leveled a professional eye at the titles. "Why, I haven't seen antiques like this in years. Zelda!" she called. "We used to have things like this in our special collection at the college, remember?"

I did remember. Old books that smelled like time and mystery. How Mom would pull one off the shelf that was too high for me to reach, and set me up at a little table with its own green glass-shaded reading lamp.

Malkin, who had disappeared into the back room, reappeared with Azure. Aloysius, Azure's golden-eyed owl, rode on her shoulder and gave everyone the stink eye.

"Well, hello to you, sir," Poppy said, wiggling her finger.

Aloysius snapped at it.

"Aloysius, behave yourself." Azure's blue robe rippled behind her and silver charms lightly jingled in her hair. "You can't seem to come to anything without a hullabaloo, can you, Zelda?"

"Afraid not," I said. "Azure, this is my mother, Effie. Mom, this is Azure Washington, Witch Presiding."

"I am so pleased to meet you, Ms. Washington."

"Please, call me Azure," the Witch Presiding said, extending her hands to clasp my mother's. "You must have had a hell of a time raising this one."

My mother laughed—the traitor. "I always say the things that drive you craziest about your children will be the things that make them the most successful."

"I'm standing right here," I muttered to Poppy.

"At least they're bonding," she said.

Mom turned to me and squeezed my arm. "You come by it honestly. I'm sure I caused your grandmother no end of trouble."

"You? Trouble?" I said. "Never."

Azure clapped her be-ringed hands together, causing Aloysius to bob up and down with alarm. "So," she said, taking a seat, "what's all this about? A ghost, in *my* swimming pool?"

"I'm afraid so," Poppy said. She repeated the story as I'd told it.

Azure listened, but kept her gaze on me the whole time. So did her owl. "And here I was thinking you had the Lord of the Blessed managed," she said, when Poppy finished.

"I did." I paused, thinking of Daniel. "I do. But no one expects the dead to come to life."

"The dead are always with us," Azure said.

"Yes, well, the dead are not always showing up on Broadway and in swimming pools. At least not in my experience."

"Your experience is largely in running restaurants," she said, mildly.

"So was my grandmother's. Didn't stop her from solving everyone else's magical problems."

Azure steepled her fingers. "And now your mother has magic, too."

"Call it the family business," I said.

"It's not very much magic," my mother added.

"She launched a fireball and melted a dozen cupcakes into slag," I said, unable to keep the pride out of my voice.

Azure gave my mother a new, appraising look.

"Look," I said. "All I want to do is figure this out. If you have something to help with that, I'm all ears. Otherwise I'll just try to stay out of your hair while we figure it out on our own."

"You and who?"

"The usual crew."

"A handful of the Blessed, a sprinkling of the Gentry, and Miss Poppy, here?"

"And me," Mom said.

"Mom, you're not getting involved."

"I'm your mother—who are you to tell me what to do?"

Azure was trying to hide a smile.

"There you have it," I said, gesturing to Poppy and my indignant mother. "The best of the best. Plus a poodle and an Irish wolfhound."

"You don't need my permission," Azure said. "We're a social club, not a governing body. However," she continued, "I'd like to keep the hostile beings—alive *or* dead—out of our building. And if you're the one who brought them in..."

"I'm the one who cleans them up," I finished.

"Precisely. But since Poppy is one of us, and we all have an interest in the general peacefulness of Manhattan, I will also put the resources of the LWW at your disposal." She gestured to the shelves.

Mom's eyes lit up. "We can borrow books?"

Azure gave a royal nod. Her owl twisted its head sideways until it looked like it might snap off.

"Great," I said. "I'll take anything you have on summoning—and banishing."

12

Poppy, my mother, and I sat in Victorine's parlor, surrounded by half a dozen open books, as Victorine paced the floor. Claudette, Victorine's housekeeper, quietly rolled in a cart of something that steamed.

"Tea, thank God," Poppy jumped up from the couch and rushed for the teapot.

"Thank you, Claudette," Victorine said, her tone both polite and indicating that we would serve ourselves.

Claudette retreated, closing the parlor doors as she went.

I flipped through *Preparing for a Seance,* a dusty book printed in 1875 that, from the looks of it, hadn't been opened since. "This says 'No person of a very strongly positive temperament or disposition should be present.' Does that mean positive like Poppy or positive like dominating?"

"If so, that's you out of the mix," Poppy said.

I ignored the crack and turned the page. "'Subdued light... open the seance with prayer or music, vocal or instrumental'... and only 'subdued, quiet, and harmonizing conversation'? What does that even mean?"

"It means," Victorine said, "the kind of conversation you're incapable of having."

I shut the book. "So you're saying I'm the opposite of everything we need to hold a successful seance?"

Victorine didn't respond. Instead, she took her time pouring a cup of tea, then gracefully sat on a side chair. "I would be saying that, if I thought a single word of that was worth the paper it was printed on."

"But these are primary sources," my mother said, holding up a copy of *The Philosophy of Spiritual Intercourse*, the title of which still made Poppy snort-laugh into her tea.

"So am I," Victorine said. "You forget that I was present for the mania of Spiritualism. I was in one of the drawing rooms when the two sisters who claimed they received messages from the beyond performed. It was all a hoax. The supposed 'tapping' of ghosts was nothing but the cracking of the sisters' joints."

"If it's all bunk, then why are we looking at it?" I said, tossing my book aside.

"Because we don't have any other ideas?" Poppy said.

I sighed and put my face in my hands, feeling my cold fingers press against my tired eyes. "I thought maybe some of this would connect to the kind of magic we *do* know: fire, or water, or air. Even if it was just a hint." I lifted my head and looked at Victorine. "Or that you would know something about the Blessed."

"I know everything about the Blessed."

"But nothing about ghosts."

"Give her tea, Poppy," Victorine said. "She is fussy, like a child."

"Not enough tea in the world to fix that," Mom said.

Everyone laughed but me. "I'm glad I amuse you all while I'm trying to banish a dangerous otherworldly monster," I said, instantly regretting how pouty I sounded. I stood up, stretched. Poppy put a cup of tea in my hand and I got a fistful of cookies for myself. "I'm sorry. I'm just frustrated. I thought this was over."

Mom came to my side and put her arm around my shoulder. "We'll fix it. Don't you worry."

"You're not supposed to be fixing it at all," I said. "You're supposed to be safe at home."

"Like I'm some kind of helpless old woman?"

"Can't I be protective?"

"Can't *I* be protective?" she fired back.

Victorine cleared her throat. "Will you be getting up to see the reverse Manhattanhenge?" she said, smoothly changing the subject.

"The what?" Mom said.

"Manhattanhenge. Named after Stonehenge. A solar event in which the sun aligns with the city grid at sunset or sunrise. If it is at sunrise, it is known as a reverse Manhattanhenge. It only happens a few times a year, and the next one is in a few days."

Mom looked delighted. "I'd love to see that."

"If you're not back at home by then," I pointed out.

"Stop ruining my fun, Zelda."

Feeling that this outing was rapidly becoming unavoidable, I addressed Victorine. "Which part of the grid does it align with?"

"44th Street, east of the library, is considered the best viewing."

At *library*, Mom's interest perked up even more. "Is that the library with the lion statues?"

"Patience and Fortitude, yes," Victorine said.

"Fine," I said. "I'll take you to see the sunrise."

Mom made a happy noise and bit into another cookie.

I swear, they get to a certain age and you can't tell who's the parent and who's the child anymore. "Now could we possibly *focus*?"

Poppy had already dived back into one of the books. "Most of it seems to be about setting the mood. There are a few objects mentioned—"

I looked up. "Oh?"

"Mirrors, for one. You wait for an apparition to appear. Or you can try to tempt them out with what's called a 'trigger object.'"

"What's a trigger object?"

Poppy finger skimmed the text. "A trigger object is an object used to lure a ghost into interacting with you. It could be something that belonged to the person, or something important to them. It can work even better, supposedly, if you are in an environment familiar to the ghost."

"Prospero's apartment," I said.

"Daniel's apartment," Victorine murmured.

"What could be a trigger object?"

While Victorine was considering, Poppy jumped in. "The sword canes!"

"Yes. Good," I said. "What else?"

"The Mirror Seal," Victorine said.

"It's in pieces," I said. "What good would that do?"

"It was the most important thing to him."

The shattered glass had made me so uncomfortable that I'd shoved it in a closet and tried to avoid looking at it. The idea of hauling it to Prospero's made the tea and cookies tumble around my stomach like it was a Kitchen-Aid mixer. "Okay…" I said. "Let's say I summon him. Great. But the point isn't actually summoning him—it's *banishing* him."

Poppy flipped ahead. "Destroy the trigger object."

"Destroy—the Mirror?" I tried to wrap my mind around destroying something so powerful, with so much history.

"It's symbolic," Poppy said. "Scares them off."

"How would you destroy it?" Mom asked.

"That's something elemental magic would work for," Poppy said. "Burn it. Melt it down."

I pictured the beautiful carvings on the empty frame, all decorated with sparkling crystal dewdrops. Burning it would be like burning art, or books. "Just the glass?"

Poppy shrugged.

I looked at our resident vampire expert. "Victorine?"

Her shrug was more elegant, but just as lacking in answers.

"Fine," I said. "Prospero's apartment. The Mirror, or what's left of it. Fire."

"Isn't this a little... off the cuff? Even for you?" Victorine said, mild as she knew how to be.

"That's how I roll."

"How reassuring."

"I'm open to other genius ideas." I looked around the room: Poppy, Mom, Victorine. Myself in the mirror, the same one I'd seen myself in that fateful day of the party. "No? Then off-the-cuff it is. Tonight."

"Tonight?" Mom said. "Are you sure?"

"I won't sleep well until I know he's six feet under, and staying put."

That night, I pulled on my jacket and added a scarf and a hat, but tucked my gloves into my pocket, leaving my hands bare. Poppy and my mother had to do one final magical top-up before I left.

"Are you sure I can't come?" Mom asked.

"What if something happened to you?" I said.

"You couldn't stop me from coming if I really tried," Mom said, drawing herself up to her full height, which wasn't much.

"I could certainly take a run at it."

"You wouldn't dare. I'm your *mother*."

"It's not just that I don't want you there—"

"A-*ha!*"

"But that he seems to show up when I'm alone."

Mom subsided, looking troubled. "I know. I understand, really." She took my shoulders and looked into my eyes. "Soon I'll be going home, Zelda, and I won't even be here to protect you. It worries me."

It meant exactly what she said but it also meant more, so much more that it suddenly hurt to swallow over the lump in my throat. "It's not that I don't want your help," I said. "It's just—I can't take the risk of scaring him off. I have to go alone."

She gave me a squeeze and a little shake before letting go of my shoulders. "At least pet the dog before you go. You said he was lucky, right?" She scooped up Jester, who had been standing between us in hopes of being included in whatever fun thing was happening.

"Is this a bad idea, boy?" I said, scratching his head. He looked at me with eyes that were simultaneously wise and absolutely clueless. "Be good," I told him. "And don't worry. I'll be back soon."

"Or I'm coming after you," Mom said, carefully setting the dog down.

"Me, too," Poppy added.

"Fine," I said. "Everyone can come after me. Now, can you unload some fire magic on me so I can do this?" I held out my hands.

They each took a hand. I closed my eyes, the better to concentrate, and focused on finding that sweet spot between passively absorbing the magic, as I usually did; and outright drawing it in, as I had done with Jessica.

I was a thick hunk of bread sopping up soup in a bowl.

Poppy's magic felt cozy and well-worn, like a velvet sofa in a pool of midday sun. Mom's magic was both new and aged, like a vintage bottle of wine that's just been opened. I took it in until my head spun with the sheer sparkling overflow of it all. "I'm good," I said, letting go of their hands.

"Call us the *minute* you get done," Poppy said.

"Yes, mother. And Mom," I said, nodding to my real mother.

She hugged me. A little more magic flowed through the embrace. Or maybe it was love.

"I'm just banishing him," I said. "I'm not doing anything dangerous."

"Be safe," she said, letting me go.

I put on my gloves and left.

Outside, the sky was already as dark and chilly as cold coffee in a black mug. Unseen clouds spat cold rain, and the lights of passing cars slid over the wet ground. I pulled my coat tighter against the night.

One too-short taxi ride later, I stood on the sidewalk and looked up at the redstone building, a dark castle only touched by a little of the warm streetlights, the lit windows less inviting and more of a multi-eyed monster peering into the darkness. Looking for me.

How many times had I gone to Gramercy Park and had my life turn on a dime?

I rode the small elevator to Daniel's floor. Everything that had already happened rode with me; everything that could happen, I tried to leave behind when I stepped into the hallway. Only the now, only the present, could come with me.

I knocked.

Footsteps, then Daniel opened the door. "Hey."

"Hey yourself," I said, stepping inside. "Where's Jessica?"

"Out." Daniel was dressed to leave: tailored slacks, polished leather shoes, a thick sweater that looked like it'd been hand-made for a millionaire. His overcoat draped the chaise lounge, and I had a brief vision of using it like a blanket, to curl up underneath and hide from everything.

"Nice sweater," I said. I didn't feel the need to flirt with him anymore, but without it, I didn't know what to say instead.

"Thanks," he said, falling silent for a moment, as if it were the same for him. "You sure you're okay to do this?"

I laughed. "I'm never sure I'm okay to do anything. And yet, here I am."

"Here you are," he said.

Oh, the silence. Like a violin string around the neck.

What were we? Friends, yes, but something else was different. Daniel, the Lord of the Blessed, and me—*untitled* but also somehow the balancing point between the witches, the Blessed, and the Gentry. It had been easier to ignore when we were simply flirting with each other to pass the time and remind ourselves how smoldering we were. Without that, we weren't just people. We were *factions*.

"Can I get you anything before I go?" he said. "A drink? Something to eat?"

"You have food?" I said, momentarily distracted from my own thoughts by the surprise. Daniel's refrigerator was usually as clean and unoccupied as Antarctica.

"Cheese—good stuff—some fruit, cold cuts, bottled water... and some fresh bread and salted nuts in the cabinet."

I stopped myself from noting out loud that he didn't actually need any of this. "Thanks," I said. "Maybe after." Unlike at any time in our long history, I wanted to set him at ease.

He seemed to want to do the same.

This friendship stuff was strange.

"I'll get out of your hair, then," he said. With that, he scooped up his coat and moved to the door. He opened the door and turned back. "I'm not going far. Call me if you need anything." Then he left.

I waited for his footsteps to fade. "Alone at last," I said to the empty room, trying to crack a joke, only to have the room suck it up like a vampire of humor instead of blood.

Time to get cooking. And if there was one thing I'd learned in cooking school, it was to make sure everything was in its place before I started: *mise en place*, as the French said.

I threw my own coat where Daniel's had been. Out of my bag, a pillowcase filled with the crumbled shards of the Mirror. The witches' copy of *Preparing for a Seance*.

I pulled a sword cane out of the stand, withdrew the blade a few inches, and snapped it back into place.

Then I went to Prospero's room.

Daniel was so neat I could have easily thought he didn't even live there. Best to go with that. *Prospero's* house. *Prospero's* room, as if those simple thoughts would summon him.

I surveyed the layout again, with a different eye than when Berron, Daniel, and I had ransacked it. I needed a place to lay the book. A place to put the broken glass. A place for the sword cane.

I propped the book on the mantel, open to a list of instructions. The sword cane and the pillowcase of Mirror fragments went on the mantel, too.

Seasoned wood and old copies of the Times lay ready next to the fireplace. I set logs and paper in place for a fire.

Returning to the open book, I read aloud: "Subdued light." I left Prospero's room and dimmed every light in the apartment for good measure. "Never let the room be overheated." I cracked a window and a cold draft sliced into the room. Opening a second window in the parlor created a freezing cross-breeze. "Prayer or music." I'd thought of playing music on my phone, but the idea seemed ridiculous standing in Prospero's room.

Instead, I went to the Victrola and looked inside the cabinet. A record already lay on the turntable: "Absence Makes the Heart Grow Fonder (Longing to Be Near Your Side)."

I turned the crank and the music crackled out of the horn.

Promise then you will not sever

From the ties that bind us two.

Say you will be mine forever,

Tell me that you still are true...

I was ready. Almost.

"Let's light it up," I said. I kneeled by the fireplace and extended my hand, palm-out. Silver magic sparked like tiny fireworks, hitting the paper and wood. Orange flames lit and smoke curled upward as the fire spread.

In my mind, Patty Melt the fire mouse stirred to life, ears and whiskers twitching.

"Hello, girl," I said, adding a few logs to the fire. "Stand by."

She hunkered down and half closed her eyes.

I straightened up and fished in my pocket, then pulled out Prospero's bow tie, the one I'd shown to Lily.

I brought it to my nose, realizing I was holding my breath against the weirdness of what I was about to do. You don't go around sniffing people's clothing without a damn good reason.

I forced myself to inhale.

Prospero's bow tie didn't smell all that different from the rest of the apartment—a little antique, a little musty, some kind of faint old-world cologne—but it was the closeness of it I was going for. The intimacy. As if I could find Prospero's ghost in the ghost of the scent he'd left behind. This was how Jester went through the world: by smell. All that information, coming through in signals that dodged the conscious brain and burrowed right down to something more instinctual.

I lowered the bow tie to my lips. "Prospero," I whispered, my breath clinging to the silk and warming it.

Meanwhile the fire warmed my feet, and the Victrola droned on.

"Come on, Prospero," I said, placing my free hand on the sword cane and concentrating harder, remembering every interaction we'd had: the charity market, the museum, the apartment, the abandoned church, the ice field.

The wind whistled and the fire danced, but no Prospero.

What would get his attention?

I set the bow tie on the mantel and picked up the bag of glass. I felt its weight—physically, but also in magic and memories—and then I carefully placed it on the fire.

The fabric burned slower than I expected, blackening and curling before disappearing into flakes of ash.

I held my hand palm-up and summoned Patty. She appeared in my hand in a burst of light and jumped into the fireplace. She seized a corner of the pillowcase and bit down, all the while glowing brighter and brighter, hotter and hotter. My borrowed fire magic shielded me from the worst of the heat but I still felt it, like the Florida sun in early September when it feels like there will never be any relief.

I turned both hands toward the fire and stoked it with magic. It couldn't burn bigger—I'd burn the building down—but within the strong old bricks lining the fireplace, I could burn it like a lighthouse beacon, strong and concentrated.

I had only as long as the fuel lasted, though. Magic could start the fire, even generate it all on its own for a while, but to go on any longer you had to have something to burn.

"Come on," I said. "Show yourself. I'm right here. Come get me."

Having incinerated the pillowcase, Patty Melt dashed in circles. The smoke and flames began to turn, then spin. The firelight dazzled my eyes till all I could see in my mind's eye was Prospero himself, dapper and sinister.

The flames were so powerful they hummed like the beehives on the roof of the Whitney museum. The fire mouse wasn't even visible, just a circular blur of furious light.

I closed my eyes. Afterimages blazed, red and orange light across the darkness.

Unbidden, unasked for, diamond-colored magic poured over me. Fire, ice, magic, and music swept away control like a fast-moving river. I was shaking uncontrollably, my hand gripping the mantel as the magic did what it wanted, transforming me against my own will.

The fire crackled like bitter laughter.

When I finally looked in the mirror above the fireplace, Prospero looked back.

Not Prospero's ghost, but his illusion—*me*, as Prospero.

I held my own red-eyed gaze. Yes, I was afraid. Yes, I wanted him gone. But as much as I wanted all of that, I needed him to hear what

I had to say. And if I had only myself to say it to, that was better than nothing.

"I'm sorry," I said, quietly. "I didn't mean for any of this to happen. I didn't mean to hurt anyone. Not even you. Even if you deserved it—I wish there'd been another way."

Over my shoulder, in the mirror's reflection, a blue haze wavered. He was behind me, a ghost of moonlit electricity.

Zelda...

My disguise faded, simply, silently, leaving the two of us reflected together in the mirror, closer and more intimate than we had ever been. "Prospero," I said, my voice barely audible.

I hardly dared move. Or breathe. Whatever I'd planned on saying before, my great plans for banishing him, turned to ashes like the pillowcase.

The fire, which had roared and buzzed only a second before, dwindled down to a lazy pop or two just to remind me it was still there.

Prospero's outline wavered. He raised his hands, and I had to stop myself from seizing the sword cane, turning, and ripping his ghost into pieces.

"Don't move," I said, trying to sound brave. The waver in my voice ruined it.

His ghostly hands rested on my shoulders. The heat fled my skin where he touched, so cold it burned. *Zelda.* His voice was firmer, as if touching me had summoned some kind of strength. *She is coming.* His eyes, so red and vivid in life, burned cold blue fire in death.

"Who is coming?" I said, already knowing, in the pit of my stomach, the answer.

You must stop her, he said, as if he couldn't even name *her*.

His form wavered, lost focus. He was falling apart.

"How?" I cried. "Tell me how!"

But it was as if his strength only stretched to a few words. *Protect them*, he said.

Then—far off—

Bells.

Prospero's head tilted back as if he was in great pain. Each pinpoint of light that outlined him pulled apart as if by a great riptide, his essence torn in silent slow motion, light devoured by darkness.

Gone.

I whirled around as if he would still be there behind me, but there was only the empty bed with its curtains blowing in the draft from the window.

He hadn't been trying to harm me.

He'd been trying to warn me.

13

The Victrola had gone silent. The sword cane lay on the mantel next to the bow tie. The fire was out, and Patty Melt looked up at me forlornly from the cooling hearth.

Somehow, I knew: no amount of flames would bring him back again.

She had stopped him.

I ran my fingers through my hair and gripped it at the roots, letting the dull pain be a sharpener for my thoughts.

Patty Melt squeaked at my feet.

When I looked down, she gently reached out a tiny paw and set one of my bootlaces on fire.

I quickly swatted the fire out. "Thanks, baby," I said. "I know you care." I scooped her up and closed my hands like a cave. Light flared between my fingers and went out, and I felt Patty Melt return.

I closed the window. Closed the Victrola. Returned to the fireplace and crouched, to survey the damage.

Inside the fireplace, the broken glass was gone. In its place, a single, sparkling drinking glass lay on the irons: pink fluted cup, hollow purple foot, and in between, the stem—holding the whole thing together—was a perfect pink glass flamingo.

I sagged to the carpet, rocking with helpless, silent, borderline hysterical laughter.

When I finally managed to pull myself upright, my stomach growled.

There might have been an interdimensional goddess on the way, preparing to destroy my soul, but even that wasn't enough to stop my hunger. Magic took it out of a person.

I remembered Daniel's snacks, and staggered to my feet.

I stumbled back to the kitchen, bringing the lights up as I went, and then I collected everything I found in the refrigerator except for the soft-sided cooler, which I suspected held blood. I didn't look.

I carried everything to the living room and laid it out on Prospero's dainty side table. It didn't all fit on one side table, so I dragged over a second one. *I should call Daniel*, I thought. *I should call Mom and Poppy. I should call Berron.*

Instead, I sat on the sofa and began mindlessly eating cheese cubes.

When I looked up from my food haze to find only empty containers, some sense returned. I typed and copied the same text to everyone: *I'm fine. Will give you more details in person.*

That should buy some time.

I dusted crumbs from my hands and leaned back on the couch, only to be interrupted by the sound of a key in a lock. I sat up and more thoroughly wiped my hands on my jeans, wondering why Daniel had come back so quickly.

The door opened.

It wasn't Daniel. It was Jessica, swathed in black: black boots, black tights, black skirt, black leather jacket, and a thick black scarf.

"How did you get back so fast?"

"I was barely a block away." She stopped in the entryway and blinked at me. "What are you doing?"

"Didn't Daniel tell you?"

"Of course Daniel told me." She approached and gave me a very unflattering onceover.

I became acutely aware of a trail of cracker crumbs down my front.

"Oh my *God*, did you eat all the food?" She picked up the empty plates and dropped them back on the side tables with a crash. "Were you raised in a *barn*?" She stalked to the kitchen and flung open the refrigerator door, peering into the depths like it was Aladdin's cave of wonders. "There's nothing *left*."

I pushed myself up and hurried to the kitchen. "Sure there is," I said, looking over her shoulder. "There's eggs and stuff—"

"For people who *cook*," she said.

The food had been stocked for her. A diet of plain old red stuff wouldn't cut it anymore, not with her powers fading. "Move and let me work," I said.

She shot me a look but budged out of the way.

I washed my hands and collected the remaining contents of the fridge. Thankfully, I hadn't scarfed *all* the cheese—there was another package unopened, so I chopped some up.

"So," Jessica said, leaning against the counter. "How did it go?"

"I had a nice chat with your old boss."

"Prospero's dead."

I hunted around for a bowl, then found a fork in a drawer. "Not as much as you might think." I washed up and began cracking the eggs, stealing a glance at Jessica. "You don't look surprised."

"He was..." She trailed off as if trying to find the right word. "I don't know." She looked sincere, for once, and it softened her face. By the time I tossed the eggshells in the trash, the hard edge was back. "Not human enough to die."

"You were his protege." I set a pan on a burner and cranked up the heat.

"I wasn't human, either." She rubbed her stomach and gave the bowl of eggs a look.

"I'm going, I'm going," I said. "You can't rush perfection." I reached for the butter and cut off a generous chunk. The butter hit the pan with a satisfying hiss and a trail of bubbles in its wake. I coated the pan and poured in the egg and cream mixture, then left it alone to solidify on the bottom.

There was a tricky maneuver you had to do when the omelet was ready to flip, but you had to time it right and do it with the perfect flick of the wrist. "Jessica," I said, "why did you dislike me so much? I mean right from the beginning, when you and James tried to kidnap me."

"Isn't it obvious?"

I gripped the pan and jerked it hard, but controlled, freeing the omelet underside from the grip of the hot pan. "Enlighten me."

"You were going to stop us from being free."

A quick upward motion, and the omelet flipped in a tight arc and landed top side down to finish cooking. "Free to prey on people outside of Manhattan?"

"Like normal people don't prey on each other." Jessica did a Gen-X eyeroll so perfect I couldn't help but smile to myself. "Is it ready yet?"

"Almost." I sprinkled cheese on the cooked side of the omelet. Only two more moves to go: a perfect fold, and then slide the completed omelet onto a plate.

"You know he asked the witches to drop the barrier."

I almost had the fold when the pan wobbled in my hand. Half of the omelet fell short, and I had to hurry to get it all the way over before it stuck in the melted cheese. "He *what*?"

"You didn't know?"

"Sometimes it feels like nobody tells me anything." I pushed the cheese omelet onto the plate, rolled a fork and knife into a napkin, and held both out to Jessica. I wondered if she'd had a pair of Doc Martens back in high school; what her favorite song had been; if we would have been friends from the start, if everything had been different. "Sorry I ate your snacks."

She looked at me for a moment, then took them. "Sorry I tried to kidnap you."

"You want to sit at the table?" I said, restaurant habits kicking in.

"Tables are for suckers," she said, stalking down the hall. "Come on." She opened her door and swept in. She dropped her phone into a stand, where it instantly began to play music.

"'Bullet with Butterfly Wings,'" I said. "A classic."

"Don't call it a classic—you're making me feel old." She flopped unceremoniously on the bed and stuffed a large bite of omelet in her mouth. "Don't just stand there. Sit down."

It was between the chair at the vanity table and the edge of the bed, so I picked the chair. Did she know we had been in here? That I had held this bottle of Poison in my hand?

"Relax," she said. "I'm not going to murder you. Besides, you could probably murder me back with your weird magic." She wiggled her fork at me. "Is that why Daniel was into you? Your powers?"

Oh, no. Not boy talk. I wasn't good at it. Strenuously avoided it, in fact. No one needed a play-by-play of the whole pint of ice cream I ate last night, either. Mistakes and pleasure should be private—especially when they overlap.

"Your silence is confirmation." She smiled wickedly. "Is he always so stuffy?"

"Not always," I said, feeling my face heat up.

"He reminds me of Prospero that way, actually," she mused.

I gazed under the bed to see if there was room for me to crawl in and hide. What did I *not* want to hear? How Daniel was like Prospero, how I was like Jessica, or any other combination that had all the appeal of a pickles and peanut butter sandwich. "Were you and Prospero... uh..."

Jessica coughed. "Together? God, no. I mean, not that I wouldn't have considered it..."

I squeezed my eyes shut. It didn't help, so I opened them again.

"But it was strictly business." She went back to the omelet.

I reached for my phone. "My, look at the time—"

"Are you seeing anyone?"

I considered jumping out the window, or possibly texting someone and saying I'd been attacked by a werewolf. *Send help.* "No, not currently."

"What about Mr. Gentry Prince? He seems like your type."

"My *type*? We've known each other for *how* long, mostly at *knifepoint*, and you think I have a *type*?"

"Sappy," she said. "Like you."

My jaw fell. "I'm not *sappy*."

She shot me a dubious look. "You're, like, a serial puppy rescuer. You can't help yourself."

"Berron is—I'm not—you—"

"Except you can't actually go for your type because then you'd have to admit you were sappy, too."

My mouth was open yet no sounds were coming out.

"That's why it didn't work with Daniel. He's a lot of things, but sappy isn't one of them," she said, blithely taking another bite of the eggs. "Are you all right? You look funny." It was almost sincere, but the wide-eyed look of concern was ruined by the mischief etched across her face.

"I'm fine," I said, standing up, hating how stuffy I sounded.

"Aren't you having fun? Isn't this what friends do?"

I was almost through the doorway when the silverware rattled on the plate and Jessica was right behind me. Grape soda and cinnamon mingled with cheese omelet when she laid her hand on my shoulder. *Poison omelet*, I thought.

"You're not mad at me, are you?"

I turned. What a weird little cat she was. No wonder I was a dog person. "No—" I started, but was interrupted by another key hitting the lock.

"Ssh," Jessica said. "Not a word to Lord Daniel. Just between us girls, right?" She winked, and I was reminded of Poppy, if Poppy were an unreliable American vampiress.

"Right..." I said.

She giggled madly, turned me around by my shoulders, and pushed me out into the hall, following right behind me.

"Hello?" Daniel called.

"We're right here," Jessica replied gleefully. We emerged into the living room and she threw her arm over my shoulder like we were old pals.

Daniel slowly removed his coat. "So I see. What happened?"

Jessica steered me over to the couch and gave me a shove so firm I lost my balance and sat. She bustled around, humming and scooping up the empty plates I'd left behind, sashaying off to the kitchen. The way she went back and forth from venom to sweetness was enough to give anyone whiplash.

Daniel cleared his throat.

"Sorry," I said, coming back to myself from yet another attempt to follow Jessica's patented weirdness. "I was able to summon Prospero."

"And?"

"The Mirror is now a flamingo drinking glass."

"I can't imagine that's all of it."

"The Arcade is coming back."

Daniel blew out a breath and sank into a chair.

Jessica reemerged from the kitchen and stood behind his shoulder, at ease, in a pose that reminded me of her second-in-command status with Prospero. She smiled at me, secretly.

"What are you going to do?" Daniel said.

"Me? I have no idea. It took a stroke of luck to defeat her last time. I doubt I could even pull the same trick twice. Not to mention that it was Prospero who set that meeting in the first place—all we did was follow him to it."

"Maybe he's just messing with you."

"He did enjoy that," Jessica added. "Messing with you, that is."

So do you, I wanted to add. "Maybe," I said. "But I get the feeling it cost him to bring me this message. Cost him enough that I don't think he's coming back."

"You don't think you could summon him again?"

I shook my head. "I know I couldn't." I knew when a pizza was cooked by the smell of it; I didn't even have to see it. This was the same. "I want Mom to go home. I don't want her here if this goes to hell." I stood and paced, trying to shake off the rising worry.

"Understandable," he said. "Do you think she'll agree?"

"I know she won't."

"Tell her if she goes back now, you'll come visit her," Jessica said.

I stopped. "That's actually not a bad idea. What made you think of that?"

Jessica shrugged. "That's what *my* mother would want."

I stared.

"What?" she said. "You people act like I didn't exist before I got initiated. You're not the only person with a mother. And—let me tell you—it gets *really hard* to explain not visiting for twenty years."

Daniel's gaze turned to her with red-glowing sympathy.

Even when Mom and I weren't getting along, I could always see her. Even if it was awkward.

The Blessed could not. Easy to believe they were too dangerous to roam, when they were midnight stories of blood and fear.

Harder when you had four of them as friends.

14

I would have had her on a flight out of JFK, Newark, or even LaGuardia the next morning, but she was too damn stubborn.

"I'm not leaving without a proper farewell," she said, in that don't-argue-with-me, I'm-your-mother tone. Also, she was currently elbow-greasing the hell out of Poppy's coffee table, in her odd habit of cleaning wherever she was an overnight guest, and it seemed rude to stop her. "Where I come from, guests don't simply vanish into the night. We show our appreciation—"

"I would *appreciate* it if you would get on a plane as soon as possible."

"Zelda." She put down the furniture polish, gripped my shoulders, and looked me in the eye. "When you're as old as I am—"

"Not this again."

"When you're as old as I am," she repeated, giving me a shake, "you realize how important it is to do things the right way. To take your time about your goodbyes and make them special."

We were both right. I wanted her out of harm's way; she wanted to cook a gigantic meal for eight people and two dogs. I had logic; she had seniority.

"Besides," she added, dropping her hands from my shoulders and looking away mournfully, "I don't know when I'll get back up here..."

Oh, *right*. She had guilt on her side, too. I'd forgotten about that. "Fine, Mother. Make your meal."

She squealed and threw her arms around me. Since I was so much taller than her, they landed mid-ribcage and made my bones creak. She released me and finished polishing nonexistent fingerprints off the coffee table. "Now," she said, "have you got a Publix around here?"

"No Publix." My mother's love for the southern grocery chain was legendary. "But we have some respectable purveyors. Or Whole Foods, if you'd prefer."

She looked at me with suspicion as she grabbed the couch pillows and fluffed them. "Whole Foods? Isn't that where all the hippies go?"

"Not anymore, Mom. It's just a grocery store, albeit a fancy one."

"Whole Foods," she muttered. "More like whole *paycheck*."

"Oh, like Publix is cheap?"

The couch pillows flew in perfect arcs and landed—*poof, poof*—in the corners, startling Jester, who had curled up in the center of the couch to take a nap while the humans barked at each other.

He leaped down, staggered slightly in mid-afternoon sleepiness, then stretched in a perfect downward dog I couldn't even dream of matching. He straightened up and trotted off to the kitchen, presumably to see if anyone had dropped food since the last time he was in there.

"And I want to use the restaurant," Mom said.

"Why can't we cook here?"

"*We* aren't cooking anything. *I'm* cooking. And—no offense—but that kitchen is sized for two or three, not six to ten." She had me there. I had almost opened my mouth to agree when she kept going. "And it was *my* mother's restaurant..."

"Yes. Fine. Whatever you want." I ended it the way all arguments with my mother eventually ended, which is why I tried not to get into them in the first place. "But we do it *tonight*, and you go home *tomorrow*. Are we clear?"

She was off humming to herself and fluffing the couch pillows again. Not listening to me in the slightest. "Mom?"

"Yes, yes, whatever you say."

"What *did* I say?"

"Something very wise, I'm sure."

Only coffee could fully drag me out of the haze of the previous night. I started with one cup at home, but made it two when I got to the restaurant.

I cooked and served and cleaned my station, letting the heat, noise, and music drown me in simple, uncomplicated sensations. It was good not to think for a while.

Until Berron burst through the door, perfectly dressed as the Brooklyn hipster who had never set foot in Brooklyn. Today's outfit had the audacity to combine corduroy slacks and a thick flannel shirt with a mustard-colored sweater over the whole thing.

Oh, and a fedora.

"Where's my sister?" he said, with all the resonance of a Broadway actor.

"Stop shouting," I said, wishing his autumn vibes outfit wasn't kind of working for me.

"She's gone."

"Gone where? She's a Princess, she can do what she wants." I finished wrapping a to-go order and slung it to James.

Berron stalked forward and faced me across the bar. "You don't understand," he said, enunciating each word. "She's never been to New York."

"So? A lot of people have never been to New York."

"Yeah, well... most of them don't think it's a good idea to carry a bow and arrows around in public. Most of them aren't used to issuing *commands*. Most of them pay attention to *traffic lights*."

"To be honest, most New Yorkers don't pay attention to traffic lights." I wiped my counter space, then glanced at Berron. He looked thunderous. "All right," I said. "Don't start throwing chairs. Not in the middle of the breakfast rush. You're worried?"

He lowered his voice. "The Princess of Arrows does not understand anything outside the Forest of Emeralds. She has never been here."

"She's heard about it enough, between you and my mother telling her tourist stories."

Berron winced.

I reached across the bar and patted his hand where it gripped the counter. "I'll help you," I said.

He swept up my hand and, cradling it in his own, pressed it with a kiss. "Thank you," he said.

My face heated, and it wasn't from the nearby grill.

A stricken look crossed his face. "I'm so sorry," he said. "I was so worried. I got carried away."

"You're—uh—still holding my hand."

"Am I?" He looked down. "So I am." He carefully laid my hand on the counter. "There." As if to prove his good behavior, or possibly remove temptation, he put his hands in the pockets of the mustard-colored sweater.

"Right," I said, looking anywhere but at him. "Let me get things squared away."

"Of course."

Somewhere in the wild, infinite universe, there was another version of me who still lived in Florida. Who worked the breakfast shift, perhaps, or maybe even slept late because she had to work the dinner shift. Who didn't get roped into finding lost Gentry princesses who had taken themselves on a field trip.

Who was seeming more and more remote, like a distant second cousin you heard someone mention once, living a life misty and far, far away.

I saluted her and her much calmer life as I pulled off my apron and hung it up.

"Leaving?" James said.

"Call Jessica in," I said.

"Do I have to?"

I ignored that. "Also," I said. "I need to see the two of you sometime. Privately. I want to try something." I got my hat, coat, and scarf, and rejoined Berron. "Where did she go, exactly?"

"That's the problem," he said. "I don't know."

"How long has she been gone?"

He pulled off his hat and ran one hand through his hair. "An hour? Maybe?"

"How much trouble could she have gotten into in an hour?"

He jammed the fedora back on his head. "I don't even want to think about it—"

We both stopped speaking as another sound cut through the air.

"That's not a normal police siren," I said. "That's some kind of alarm."

We hurried outside. The sound was much louder than it had been inside the shop, and on the sidewalk it was easy to determine that it was coming from the east, toward Central Park.

I looked at Berron. "You don't think..."

"It's her," we both said. And we took off running, full speed.

Even when you have magic that lets you run flat-out without tiring, cold breaths still burn going in. Multiply that effect over a few blocks, and by the time we came within sight of the New-York

Historical Society and the American Museum of Natural History, it was like I'd been inhaling Tabasco sauce.

The screeching alarm ricocheted off all the buildings as if it was coming from every single one of them. "Is it one of the museums?" I puffed. "Which one?"

"Which one has more jewels?"

"I mean, the Natural History museum is mostly animals, right?"

"Don't forget the hall of gems and minerals," he said, his shoes hitting the pavement in a steady run.

"Damn, I forgot about that."

"But the other one has a gem exhibition right now, too."

A milling crowd in front of the New-York Historical Society put an end to the debate.

"If she's in one of her golden gowns, she should be pretty hard to miss," I said.

We made our way through the crowd.

"What if they've arrested her or something? What am I going to do?"

"Hush. There's a guard."

We approached the entrance.

"Back, please. Stay back," said the guard.

"What's going on?" I said.

"I can't give out any information on that."

"Come on, man, this guy's sister was in there. He's worried." I grabbed Berron's shoulder, to inspire sympathy but also to hold Berron back in case he decided to grab the guard by the throat.

The guard's face softened a little. "It's an ongoing investigation, ma'am—"

"Did you see," Berron said, his voice resonating so warmly it hummed the stone steps beneath our feet, "a woman in gold?"

Sweat appeared on the guard's forehead. "I—uh—"

"We should be allowed to go in," Berron pressed.

I silently hoped the man wouldn't have a concussion from the sheer force of Gentry power Berron was bringing to bear.

"Yeah," the guard said, looking slightly sick. "You two go on in."

"Thank you," Berron said. He touched his finger to the brim of his hat and gave the guard a charming smile.

The guard smiled back, but sweat dripped down his forehead.

We ran up the entrance steps. "How long will that work on him?" I said.

"Long enough."

"If you *ever* do anything like that to me, I will make sure you die a painful death."

"Do you want to find my sister, or do you want to yell at me?"

"Why not both?" I said, stopping at the entrance door and peeking through the glass. There was no one in the lobby; presumably, they were further in, where the action was. "Come on." I pulled the door open and followed Berron inside.

The cold stone floor and the empty lobby made our steps echo.

"Go ahead, magic yourself up and go see what happened," Berron said.

"'Magic myself up?'"

He made an aristocratic handwave in my direction. "Disguise yourself."

"As what, exactly?"

"That curator you pretended to be last time."

"What if she's there?"

"Run away fast."

I gave him a look.

"Or be the security guard we just saw. I don't know. Just get in there and find out what happened."

From farther down the hall came an animated one-sided conversation I couldn't quite make out. I motioned him to silence, and listened. "It's the curator," I said. "The one who knows Victorine." I paused, considering the options. "I'm not going to disguise myself. I'm going to go talk to her."

"What if she thinks you're in on whatever happened?"

"*Then* I run away fast."

We continued down the hall in the direction of the voice.

"There's an *arrow* in the *wall*," the curator said. She paused, seeming to listen. "Of course I'm sure! How could I be unsure about an arrow in the wall?"

Berron and I rounded the corner into the gallery.

The curator stood at the other end of the room, her back to us. Between us and her stood an assortment of pillars topped with clear rectangular cases.

The case closest to the door contained a tiny gold ostrich statue with gemstone eyes. Pearls and gold ornaments covered its gold-feathered tail. A gemstone bow tie perched on the golden bird's long neck. The knick-knack could have fit in my hand, and probably would have paid for a second location of West Side Sandwiches.

As we walked on, something crunched under my feet.

Glass. It was everywhere, in small rectangular pieces.

"Who's there?" the curator said.

"It's Zelda Hawkins," I said, following the glass trail like breadcrumbs to an empty pillar.

"I should have known," she said. "And who's your friend?" she added, taking in Berron's height, his looks, and his mustard-colored sweater.

"Him?" I said, glancing at Berron as if he had only just appeared. "He's my secretary."

Berron had a coughing fit.

"I suppose you have something to do with this, then?" She gestured to the wall, where a golden arrow had been deeply embedded. "Look at it. Went right through the case and shattered it."

Berron recovered and reached for the arrow, only to be stopped by the curator.

"Don't touch it," she said. "We'll need it for fingerprints."

"I don't think you'll find those in any database," he said.

I leaned down and read the small informational card attached to the column. "The *Heavy Heart*. 'A small lamp consisting of an eighteen carat gold wheelbarrow decorated with colored diamond flowers and holding a large citrine heart.' How large, exactly?"

"Several inches across."

I whistled.

She cupped both hands together. "And the night light itself is this much solid eighteen carat gold."

"Talk about sweet dreams." I said. A golden wheelbarrow with a golden gem for a golden princess. It made sense, in a Gentry sort of way.

"For some reason," the curator added, interrupting my thoughts, "when you people show up, things seem to go missing."

"'You people'?" Berron said.

I elbowed him. "We'll find it," I said. "Come on." I grabbed Berron and we went back outside.

Berron dropped onto one of the green benches and began bouncing his knees rapid-fire in a fit of nervous energy. "'You people,'" he muttered.

"Berron, focus. If you were a Gentry princess with a heavy decorative item, what would you do next?"

"How should I know? Even I don't fire arrows through museum displays."

A savory scent wafted through the air: New York hot dogs. "Those hot dogs smell good."

"Is this about your stomach or finding my sister?"

I grabbed his arm and dragged him along. "Maybe she got hungry."

"But she doesn't have any money—"

"No, she has a solid gold knick-knack to trade."

Berron came to a stop with a look of horror. "She wouldn't need to trade it."

"What do you mean? Why?"

"You'll see."

This time, he grabbed *my* arm and dragged *me* along.

15

We followed the sidewalk along the edge of Central Park, stopping at each of the vendors and asking if they'd seen a girl dressed in gold.

No, no, and no. Shaken heads. Uninterested faces.

We reached the last cart in the area and Berron stepped up. "Hey, have you seen a teenage girl dressed all in gold? She order a hot dog from you?"

The hot dog seller's expression crumpled like the aluminum wrappers he put on the dogs. "Why you wanna know?"

"Just answer the question."

"I ain't gotta answer no questions from the likes of you. Order or move along, you're scaring off business." He waved a thick hand.

"She bought one, didn't she?" Berron said. "Let me see the money she gave you."

"What is this, some kinda scam? I said beat it!"

"Zelda, give the man some money for his atrocious dirty water dogs."

"Me? Why not give him *your* money?"

"Because I don't have any."

I glared at Berron and pulled out my wallet. "Two, please," I said.

"Oh, and a couple of bottled waters," Berron added.

I shoved him.

"What?" he said. "I'm thirsty."

"Be thirsty on your own budget."

The hot dog man dutifully prepared two dogs and pulled two bottled waters out of a cooler.

Berron collected the food and cold drinks. "Listen, man. My sister? She's... kind of a troublemaker. We try to keep a close eye on her but"—he shrugged—"you know how it is with family."

Against all odds, the hot dog man was actually nodding.

"Anyway, sometimes she gets some fake cash and tries to spend it with unsuspecting innocent businesspersons like yourself."

"Fake? You mean like counterfeit?"

Berron nodded.

The man rooted around in a cash box. "She gave me a twenty. I marked it with the counterfeit pen and everything." He held up what appeared to be a completely normal twenty-dollar bill and squinted at it.

While the hot dog seller was performing this careful inspection, Berron quietly took my hand.

"What are you—"

"Ssh." His magic climbed my arm like the ivy climbed the walls in my bedroom: persistent, green, and smelling of spring. As it sank in, the completely normal twenty-dollar bill faded from green to a very abnormal rust color.

Then it became, simply, a big leaf.

I gasped.

"Sir, I can tell that bill's a fake," Berron said. "If you'll return it to me, I'll give you a real one."

Suspicion soured his face like pickled onions. "You think I'm going to give this to you just because you say it's a fake."

Berron sighed. "Nevermind. Keep it." He turned to me. "Give him a twenty."

"This date is getting wildly expensive," I said, pulling another bill out of my wallet and passing it over the counter.

"See?" Berron said. "We paid you back for what my sister did. No harm done. Now, did she say anything to you? Anything at all?"

The hot dog man tucked the bill away safely. "She said she wanted to go shopping. That's pretty much what you would expect from a teenager, eh?" He laughed. "How does a teenage girl not know where to go shopping?"

"Did you make any suggestions?"

"I told her to try the Columbus Circle mall. My nieces like to go there when they're in town. I said, 'All you gotta do is walk south along Central Park West until you see the pointy statue.' Then she left." He heaved a big, philosophical shrug.

"Thank you," I said.

We walked on.

"You want any of this?" Berron said, brandishing our very expensive snack.

"Leave the dogs, keep the waters."

"What?" he said, chucking the hot dogs in a trash can. "Too good for street meat?"

"I don't see you chowing down."

"I'm a vegetarian," he said. "I wouldn't eat them if they were from Nathan's on Coney Island."

"You're missing out. Although personally I think Gray's Papaya has it all over Nathan's. Nathan's is just coasting on reputation at this point. If you want a dog from a cart, though—"

"I don't."

"Shut up, you might learn something. If you want a cart dog, there's a guy who sells 'em out front of the Met. Marine veteran. Fought the city to get that spot. Good story." I swigged the water until half of it was gone.

Berron drank some of his. "I've never been to Coney Island."

I almost said, *Eh, you're not missing much*, but I swallowed it along with another sip of water. It had been too easy to take for granted how easily I could go where I wanted, anytime I wanted. If I were trapped in the same twenty-two square miles forever, Coney might sound pretty good. "Maybe we'll go there someday," I said. "I'll buy you a funnel cake, and you can throw it up after you ride the Cyclone."

"And then to Sparkle Beach," he said, getting into it. "Where I will bathe in Suntan Queen lotion and fry myself to even more of a crisp than a funnel cake."

"You remember Sparkle Beach and Suntan Queen? I think I've mentioned them to you, like, once."

Berron looked offended. "I *listen*, Zelda."

I smiled to myself, a little, picturing Berron in swim trunks and a floatie, with a stripe of brightly colored zinc sunscreen down his nose.

When we reached Columbus Circle, traffic had slowed to a crawl—and not from rush hour. The massive roundabout had five lanes circling a small island of concentric flowerbeds and a ring of fountains, all framing a marble statue of Christopher Columbus atop a tall pillar decorated with boats. The usual swirl of movement had been slowed by a car that had managed to jump the curb and hit a direction sign on the edge of the island.

A crowd of onlookers had joined in the owner's effort to push the car off the bent sign, where it appeared to be stuck.

Berron surveyed the scene. "You'd have had to make a real effort to swerve hard enough to leave the innermost lane and make it onto the sidewalk."

"Probably avoiding hitting your sister, who walked into traffic," I said.

He nodded solemnly. "Better go get her before she tries to cross again."

We joined the rush of pedestrians crossing to the closest side of the monument island. Chris Columbus loomed overhead, attracting pigeons with nothing better to do. We reached the other side of the island and waited our turn to cross the traffic circle again.

The mall itself rose in layers of steel beneath a bank skyscraper. It reminded me of Daniel and his condo: modern, polished, money. The glass-fronted atrium towered many stories above, each shop window promising a different brand name famous for luxury, while escalators carried passengers below street level to an upscale grocery store.

We stopped in front of a mall directory.

"Where do we even look?" I said. Then I thought of the leafy fairy money she'd given the hot dog vendor. "And how do we cover what she bought? I can't cover a shopping spree at Whole Foods, let alone Burberry."

"Maybe she hasn't bought anything yet." Even Berron didn't sound like he believed himself.

"At least she already has a knick-knack, so maybe she'll leave Swarovski alone."

"Very funny."

"I think we can safely rule out Hugo Boss, unless she's shopping for you."

"More like Daniel," Berron scoffed.

"Williams-Sonoma? Is she really into kitchenware?"

"Whole Foods," he said. "It smells kind of like home."

We took the down escalator at a jog, dodging around stationary riders to descend below street level.

The polished concrete floors shone under the carefully aimed spotlights. Everything, from the flower stand to the immense piles of produce, looked artfully placed and perfect. Almost *too* perfect. I liked food, and I liked quality, but something about Whole Foods made me want to topple a display just to mess it up a bit. I preferred the Union Square Greenmarket with its jazzy chaos.

We started at the produce section. It's not like the Princess of Arrows could have been hiding there—the displays were low enough to reveal anyone but a small child—but when you look for something, you have to stop and really pay attention.

The nearby flower stand almost overwhelmed the scent of fruits and vegetables, but not quite. The crisp, sweet smell of apples was in the air. Traces of dirt on the humble Russet potatoes and their fancier multi-colored cousins. The green of cut cucumbers in boxed salads. Oranges and lemons in piles.

And yet... there was something else. Something green but not fleshy; not cucumbers, not cut bell peppers for fajitas, not torn lettuce slowly wilting in a salad bag. A growing green. A living green. A *wild* green. Where had I smelled that before?

Something, in this place of perfect order, was out of place.

The produce lay before me like one of those cartoon pictures in the newspaper: *spot the difference.*

I stalked the aisles. Celery, green beans, cut herbs. Kiwi, onions, bananas. What was I missing? And why did it seem so familiar?

I completed the circuit and came back to the apple ziggurats.

And then I saw it—

A bite mark.

I hurried forward and scooped up the bitten apple. A delicate bite, taken out of the reddest and best part.

And not only that, but the apple itself had sprouted leaves! Tiny, emerald leaves blooming freshly on a stem no longer stiff. Every apple surrounding the bitten one had sprouted them too. The familiar smell? Riverside Park, with its wild apple trees. Not just the fruit, but the leaves.

"Berron!" I called, hurrying to the next apple bin and finding another bitten apple surrounded by a halo of more apples with green leaves. Almost every variety had been sampled: Cosmic Crisp, Sugar Bee, Autumn Glory.

Almost. She'd skipped Red Delicious, and who could blame her?

I gathered the bitten apples into my arms until they threatened to spill onto the floor, at which point I had to use my shirt as a makeshift basket.

Berron walked up. "What are you doing? This is no time to be shopping."

I fumbled an apple out of my collection and shoved it in his face. "Look. Your sister was here."

He peered at the apple. He took it out of my hand and brushed his thumb over the new green leaves.

He was holding his other hand, the one not holding an apple, behind his back.

I looked over his shoulder. "You were getting a *coffee*? I thought you said this was no time to be shopping."

"I think better with caffeine."

"Give me that." I took it out of his hand and downed a scalding sip, then handed it back. "There. Now we're both thinking better." I dumped the apples out of my shirt onto the nearest pile. "How many checkouts are open?"

"Just one. It's not busy."

I grabbed one of the apples. "Let's buy it and see if there are any leaves in the cash drawer."

We headed for the checkout.

When the cashier rang up the apple—now looking the worse for wear, having been picked up, bitten, put down, sprouted, and picked up again—the drawer sprang open to accept my money and revealed a couple of leaves stacked on top of the one-dollar bills. "Bingo," I said.

"Pardon?" the cashier asked.

"Did you happen to see a young woman dressed all in gold a little while ago? Carrying a bow and a quiver full of arrows maybe?"

"Yeah, you know her? What is she, some kind of street performer?"

"Yeah, she's a, um, street performer. Trouble is, I wanted to catch her next show but she didn't tell me where she was going. Did she mention anything to you?"

"She didn't say anything. Just bought a paper." The cashier gestured to a rack.

I scooped one up. "I'll take one, too."

"One apple, one paper. You want a bag?"

I shook my head and took my items, and then we walked out. "Does she read the paper? Is there a *Forest of Emeralds Times*?"

"Beats the hell out of me; and no," Berron said as we ascended the escalator.

"Where to next?" I said when we stepped off.

"I can't just go home and sit on my hands," he said. Frustration gave him wrinkles around his eyes. I could have traced them with the tip of my little finger, like scores on a peanut butter cookie. "Maybe we should—"

"Hang on," I said, stopping him with one hand. A familiar silhouette had caught my eye in the store across the way.

The sign over the door said Venus et Fleur, and the windows were filled floor to ceiling with colorful displays of dozens of roses stuffed neatly into boxes. Round boxes, square boxes, even heart-shaped boxes.

The familiar silhouette became Victorine, chic as usual in an elegant outfit that I couldn't pull off even if I hired an army of stylists. She held a box of red roses in her hands and examined it carefully. "Victorine!" I called as Berron and I entered the flower shop. "What are you doing here?"

Victorine spoke without even turning to look. "I suspect that I live here, Zelda. And occasionally, I do some shopping." She put the box down, finally, and faced us. "Berron," she said, with a nod.

"Victorine."

"And you?" Victorine said. "Are you also doing some shopping? I confess that Columbus Circle is a poor destination; you would do better by far on Fifth Avenue."

Berron picked up the box of bright red roses that Victorine had put down, and brought it to his nose. He made a face. "They're dead!"

"Indeed they are," Victorine replied. "Which is what brought me here, rather than to one of my usual stops."

I took the box from Berron. The roses were beautifully arranged, brightly colored, and definitely dead. "Why would anyone want dead roses?"

"It is most difficult to buy a gift for a wealthy person, as you can imagine. What do you buy the person who has everything?"

"Not dead stuff," Berron muttered.

Victorine ignored him. "Instead we purchase novelty." She gestured to the boxes of dried roses. "Flowers that will last forever. Or close enough."

"Who's it for?" I said.

"A normal person would not ask."

"Who said I was normal?"

A faint smile moved her lips. "A housewarming gift for the new Lord of the Blessed. I have been remiss in welcoming him. I thought a box of 'Eternity' flowers would be suitable."

"The new Lord of the—oh! You mean Daniel," I said.

"I can't get anything past you, can I?" She leaned in, peering at the paper tucked under my arm. "Did you pick that up off the bench?"

"What bench?"

"Someone left a paper on the bench by the entrance. I assumed you picked it up, to save a dollar."

Berron and I looked at each other. "No..." I said.

"Ah, well," she said, turning away to examine another expensive box of dead flowers. "Someone will pick it up soon enough."

"Good luck with Daniel's roses," I said. "Excuse us, will you?"

"Au revoir," Victorine said, without looking.

I dragged Berron away.

"What's the rush?" he said.

"What if it's your sister's paper?"

"So?"

"Maybe there's a clue!"

We reached the bench and Berron scooped up the paper. He unfolded it and handed me half. We sat side by side, and the scent of apple mixed with newsprint rose as we flipped pages.

"I've got something," he said, pulling out a sheet. A large piece had been torn from it. "Get your copy and see what's on this page."

I quickly unfolded mine and found the page. What my copy had, and the other did not, was a photograph of the Statue of Liberty illustrating an article about a local protest.

"The Statue of Liberty?" Berron said. "But she can't get there—it's outside the barrier."

"Battery Park," I said. "Anyone she asks will say Battery Park. That's where the tours depart from."

"Did you find what you were looking for?" Victorine stood before us, her dark sunglasses and silk scarf in place, a large, fancy-looking Venus et Fleur bag in her hand.

"Do you have your car?" I said.

"Why?" The word was long, drawn-out, laced with a century of suspicion and a less-than-charitable view on human nature in general.

"We need a ride to Battery Park."

16

Victorine dropped us off on South Street along the edge of Battery Park. Trees rose from the interior, marking the distance with crowns of green, yellow, and flame. We passed the usual sidewalk vendors and entered the park itself on a path that curved around trees and beds of plants. A salty wind blew off the harbor and made fallen leaves tumble past.

"She's here," Berron said.

"How do you know?"

"How do you know when the bread's done?"

A small building shaped like the crown of a pointed silver seashell rose on our right. Inside, glowing shapes dipped and swirled, and faint, dreamy music carried on the harbor breeze. "What's that?" I said.

"SeaGlass Carousel. Never been on it?"

"Not sure I'd fit on the kiddie carousel."

The path branched to the left and right, but we continued straight toward the blue water of the harbor. In between the trees, old-fashioned lamp posts rose, and beyond them, a tall ship bobbed at anchor. Further down, a more modern ferry from the Statue of Liberty released its passengers onto the promenade.

"I don't see her," I said.

We both turned slowly, scanning the broad walkway.

"There." He pointed toward the ferry.

I caught a flash of gold fabric rippling along the edge of a bench facing the water. It was the Princess of Arrows, lying down, with one arm draped over her forehead. Her quiver and her bow lay on the ground beneath the bench, and she'd propped something shiny on her stomach that winked a yellow more golden than the autumn trees.

"Is she okay?" I said.

Berron said nothing as we hurried past the tall ship, toward the ferry. "Sister," he said, when at last we stood over the Princess of Arrows, "are you ill?"

The Princess slowly removed her arm from over her eyes. She shaded them with her hand instead, and looked up at us, seemingly unsurprised by our presence. "I thought it would be bigger," she said.

"What would be bigger?" I said. I, for one, couldn't take my eyes off the treasure she was casually cradling on her stomach: a wheelbarrow crafted of gold, carrying a huge yellow gemstone carved in the shape of a faceted heart.

She followed my gaze. "Not that," she said. "The statue." She gestured in the direction of the harbor, where the Statue of Liberty did indeed look tiny, far off between Governor's Island and Ellis

Island. "Here," she said, handing off the priceless museum piece to Berron like it was a cheap souvenir snowglobe, and picking up the scrap of newspaper it had held in place. She held out the picture of the Statue of Liberty to me. "See?"

"It *is* big," I said. "You just have to get on a ferry to see it up close."

"I tried," the Princess said. "But the closer I got to the water, the more faint I became. I had to lie down, as you can see."

"The barrier," Berron said, still examining the gemstone heart in the golden wheelbarrow.

"I should like to see it up close," the Princess said, following the thought with a great sigh. "I suppose I never shall."

Berron handed me the museum's property. It was even heavier than it looked, and I almost fumbled it. Instead, I lost my grip on the newspaper clipping and it spun away in the wind, gone forever. I adjusted my grip on the base of the wheelbarrow, avoiding where tiny tufts of gold grass and miniature gemstone flowers threatened to scratch my hands.

"Sit up, Princess of Arrows," Berron said. "It is no good lounging in sadness."

"But I cannot lounge in joy, brother."

"Nevertheless," he said, taking her hands and pulling her to a sitting position, "we must try."

She swung her feet down to the ground, making space on either side of her. Berron sat to her left, and I to her right. The three of us stared out at the Statue of Liberty.

I was the only one who would ever climb to her crown.

I hefted the little wheelbarrow and desperately wished to change the subject. "No wonder they call it the *Heavy Heart*," I said.

"Do you know the story?" the Princess asked. "It is from an old tale of unrequited love: a heart that became so heavy it had to be carried in a wheelbarrow."

Suddenly I found the far off Statue of Liberty fascinating. Anything was preferable to looking at Berron.

"In that sense the gemstone heart is not heavy enough," she said. "It is a light thing, compared to the weight of wanting something you cannot have."

The sailing ship slipped free of the dock and glided away.

I cleared my throat. "We may not be able to climb the Statue of Liberty, but there are plenty of fun things to do here—didn't we see a carousel back there?" I widened my eyes at Berron, hoping he would take the hint.

He met my gaze. The flash of sadness in it could have been the changing light on the water, for it was gone in an instant. He smiled and patted his sister's hand. "You would like it very much," he said.

"Would I?" she replied, still watching the sailing ship as it got smaller and smaller. Another sigh, then she turned to me. "Would I like it, my dear friend?"

I nodded with more enthusiasm than I'd ever in my life shown for a kiddie ride.

The Princess of Arrows stood. She gathered up her quiver and arrows. Her gaze lingered over the harbor, taking in all the places she couldn't reach, and her golden gown fluttered in the breeze. Then she turned. "I am quite ready," she said.

We left the harbor behind and retraced our steps through the park, to the little silver building with the conical, shell-like roof.

The tickets ate up another bite of my cash-on-hand, and we entered the building itself to wait our turn.

Each carousel vehicle was shaped like a fish, with a circular cutout in the middle to hold a single rider. The fish glowed from within in a soothing ocean palette of colors: muted blue, soft green, lemony gold, blush pink. They dipped and rose, turned and revolved, to a soundtrack of dreamy, drifting music.

Our tickets were large, on heavy cardstock, and embossed with a sea creature beneath the name of the carousel. In a city where so many receipts and tickets were printed on disposable laser-print paper, or not printed at all, this ticket could have been framed and put on the wall. I caught Berron running his thumb over the embossed ridges, and for some reason, goosebumps rose on my arms.

The gate opened and we split up.

I climbed into a fish, and the ride began.

Berron, the Princess of Arrows, and I swirled past each other as the spinning floor made our fish swim in unpredictable paths.

When Berron's golden fish spun toward mine, I had to stop myself from reaching out. A child's impulse, maybe; to touch hands before you are taken away, even for just a moment, from someone. Why was it I could stand next to him all afternoon, and not even think of touching him, and then I get on a carnival ride and my fingers itch?

I gripped the *Heavy Heart* on my lap harder. I didn't want to be the one to have to explain to the curator why the *Heavy Heart* was now a broken one.

After a few minutes, the fish slowly spun to a stop. The Princess of Arrows was smiling as she alighted from her fish vehicle. "Most enjoyable," she said.

"We should go to the urban farm, too," Berron said as he joined us.

"Shouldn't we get your sister home?"

The Princess turned her gaze on me. "Why?"

"I thought... you might be, uh, tired?" I'd chased this Gentry runaway from the Upper West Side to Lower Manhattan and yes, damn it, I was tired. I hadn't been topped up by any of my magical stamina-filled friends in a while. When Berron took my wrist at the hot dog cart, it was barely a dash of magic.

"My dear friend," she said, placing an elegant hand on my arm. "Doing nothing fatigues me. This"—she gestured around us—"is most invigorating." She walked on with a little hop and a skip.

I wilted a little, feeling very human in comparison.

"Hey." Berron leaned closer to me. "Are you tired?"

"No."

He raised an eyebrow.

I sighed and gave up the pretense of being Superwoman. "Yes."

He chuckled. "May I hold your hand as we walk?"

"Yeah." I ran my hand through my hair. So casual. So unaffected. Good job, Zelda.

Then I took his hand.

It means nothing, really, to hold hands. It's just skin pressed against skin. The sensation is warm and comfortable, true. But in the vast scheme of things what does it really *do*? Does it change the world? No. You can't hold hands forever. It's a unity that's there one moment, gone the next.

And yet...

We are together, Berron and I, as our hands clasp; as his magic revives me; as the harbor breeze comes from behind and whips our hair in the wrong direction, blinding us both until we stumble into each other, laughing.

There is something I am beginning to feel that isn't hunger, isn't passion, isn't any of the easy and straightforward needs of the body. It is strong but it weakens me, like the urge to cry. I don't *want* to let go of his hand—and that's what *makes* me let go.

Berron looked at me. "Did you get enough?"

"Much better, thank you." I silently congratulated myself on not actually answering.

The Princess of Arrows had beaten us to the farm and was already flitting up and down the rows. I'd expected to see empty rows covered in straw or leaves—but there were a surprising number of green plants still standing tall. "They're still growing things," I said. "In November!"

"Winters are milder than they used to be," Berron said.

I scoffed. "What I know about farming could be written on the back of a SeaGlass carousel ticket."

"What's to know? Soil, water, sunshine, air…"

"Easy for you to say. You have all the plant magic."

"So do you, now. Here," he said, kneeling in the nearest row and patting one of the raised beds. "Come see."

I didn't mind getting dirty in pursuit of just about anything indoors—when you clean working kitchens, you've seen the worst of it, short of bathrooms—but real soil made me hesitate.

"Scared of a little dirt?"

I told him to do something anatomically impossible to himself, then dropped down beside him and set the *Heavy Heart* on the end of the row. Hopefully, no one would steal it while I was talking to plants.

"Now," he said, "put your hand on the ground."

"How is this different from what we do in Gramercy Park?"

"God, you're difficult." But he was smiling as he took my hand and laid it flat on top of the bed. "Close your eyes."

I rolled them first.

"What do you feel?"

"I *feel* self-conscious." But he had all the patience to wait for me to take it seriously, so I stopped kidding around and actually tried to focus.

The dirt was cold, stealing the warmth from my hand. The aroma of soil and fallen leaves mixed with the saltwater breeze. A deep vibration suddenly hummed through my legs and my hand. "Is that—"

"The subway."

I pushed the sensation aside and sent my borrowed Gentry magic into the ground. Regularly spaced splotches of magic appeared in my vision like footlights on a Broadway stage. "There's something in there. Bulbs?"

"Garlic."

I leaned closer to the ground and let my chef's senses take over. Sure enough, I could smell it.

"They'll come up in the spring."

I nodded, still with my eyes closed, still sensing the network of life that ran under our feet. Then I released a little of my own magic to embrace the sleeping plants. "Am I doing it right?"

Berron said nothing at first, but his magic bloomed around mine, echoing and strengthening. "Perfect."

I opened my eyes. "Can we do this for the whole farm?"

Berron's eyes were sparkling. He stood and offered a hand. "Let's do it."

Neat labels identified the plants, and Berron told me more: carrots, spinach, and collard greens that were cold-hardy enough to last the winter; blueberries, mint, sunchokes, asparagus, and fig trees that would die back and return. Over all of them we cast the Gentry's protection and strength, to feed the community when warmth returned.

The Princess of Arrows added her own spell, like green and gold fireflies darting among the rows.

In the way that Berron stood—as if this place had *meaning*, as if it was as much his home as the Fortress of Apples; not just a hopeless little plot in a city of steel and concrete, but a beacon of what could be right and true—I could see him for the prince that he was. It made me want to lean against him. To try out letting someone else hold me up. Letting *Berron* hold me up.

But the clash of sea glass chimes stopped me.

"Are there windchimes here?" I said.

Berron gave me a funny look. "No..."

The chimes trailed into glassy laughter. From its perch on the ground, the golden yellow gem of the *Heavy Heart* seemed to tremble.

"I should go," I said. "I need to get ready for the big dinner."

17

The kitchen brigade consisted of Mom, James, Jessica, and me. We'd pushed the tables together so everyone could fit: Poppy, Lily, Victorine, Daniel, Berron, and the Princess of Arrows. Since Lily was present, everyone pretended to be normal.

Or as normal as they could manage.

Poppy had a handful of dog treats and kept everyone entertained by running Jester and Georgiana through their tricks. Jester could sit, beg, shake hands, high-five, and spin in a circle. Georgiana could "dance" on command by putting her paws on Poppy's shoulders.

Victorine and Daniel, seated next to each other, looked like the king and queen in a pack of New York-themed playing cards.

Berron wore his usual hepcat gear, but must have been unable to convince the Princess of Arrows to abandon her shimmering gold getup for something less unusual. Not surprisingly, Lily spent a long time ooh-ing and ah-ing over the fabrics—gold velvet, gold chiffon, gold-embroidered linen—until I was pretty sure Lily might convince her to swap clothes in the kitchen pantry.

Berron, in the way he had of being either the most noticeable person in the room or the most hidden, chose to fade into the background. His eyes took in everything, as usual. Including me, when he thought I wasn't looking.

When I caught him at it, he gave me a small salute and an almost-smile.

Admiration, quiet enough for me to handle.

If by the end of yesterday I'd been tempted to rest my head on his shoulder, to *stop* for a moment, to *let go*, I had resisted admirably. Although *why* it was admirable was beginning to become hazy, like trying to see the Statue of Liberty through smog. "Coca-Cola ham ready?" I said to Mom.

"Almost," she said, readjusting the garnishes.

Jessica, who had shown close to zero interest in working with anything savory, had developed a fixation on pastry. She stood at the other end of the kitchen in an all-black kitchen outfit, meticulously putting the finishing touches on an apple spice cake frosted with fall-colored leaves.

I had once tried pointing out, in a friendly way, that her artistic background came in handy. She just gave me a patented Jessica death stare and walked away.

Her new hobby kept her out of James's hair, anyway. He was always more of a line cook kind of guy. He was currently preparing garnishes for the twice-baked potatoes: individual ramekins of sour cream, bacon, and finely chopped chives.

The Princess of Arrows rose from her chair and tapped a spoon on her glass. We didn't have sapphire-berry juice on tap, so it was filled with iced cranberry juice instead. When everyone turned, her serene smile beamed over us all. "I wish to give a toast," she said. "To thank all of you for making me welcome."

I cut a look at Berron, hoping this wasn't going to be anything she shouldn't say, but he gave me a hidden thumbs-up to say *It's okay.*

Lily leaned over to me. "Where did you say she was from?"

"Upper East Side. Old money," I whispered back. A close-enough excuse for her rare-orchid behavior.

The Princess of Arrows delicately cleared her throat. "May your heart never be heavy, for your friends will lift it. May your harvest ever be plenty, for your friends will share it. Though worlds and seasons change, we will drink to what remains: friendship." She took a dainty sip of cranberry juice, then puckered her lips and laughed.

Everyone drank.

"Hear, hear!" Berron said.

She blushed, curtsied, and sat.

"Dinner is served!" Mom said. She hefted the Coca-Cola ham and carried it to the table. "Of course, we call it 'supper' where I come from."

"Dinner, supper," I said. "Who cares? Smells delicious." I delivered side dishes of twice-baked potatoes, green bean casserole, and baskets of gluten-free bread warm from the oven. James dropped off garnishes and butter.

Lily's eyes sparkled at the sight of everything on the table being safe for her to eat.

Jessica, who had been lingering in the kitchen, removed her apron and headed for the empty spot next to Daniel. He immediately stood and held her chair while she sat.

Poppy grabbed the pre-made plates for the dogs—nothing that would give either of them indigestion—and set them on the floor nearby.

The Gentry loaded their plates with the sides.

The Blessed could eat, even if they didn't exactly crave food the same as they craved the red stuff, so they picked and choosed according to individual preference. Victorine, as usual, took barely anything. Jessica, on the other hand, had as much of an appetite for eating the savory food as she had a dislike for cooking it.

"You can't tell it's gluten-free," Poppy said after a bite of fresh bread and salted Irish butter. "It tastes just like regular bread. Simply marvelous!"

"You're not eating," Daniel said to my mother.

She laughed. "I was too busy watching y'all eat."

"Me, too," I said. Something else we apparently had in common. I handed her a plate and took one for myself. When I finally sat down and looked around the table, I almost wished my mom *wasn't* going home. I'd never pictured her in New York, not really—but from Broadway to the Forest of Emeralds, she fit right in. There was so much more I wanted to show her, too. Maybe next time my idiot brother could show up and we could really set the town on fire.

After the meal, while Jessica was plating dessert, I snuck off to the back room. I hauled potatoes out of the way to access a plain cardboard box I'd hidden deep in one of the shelves. I took the box down, tore the packing tape off the top, and gazed down at the contents.

Brand, spanking-new West Side Sandwiches ball caps with an updated logo designed by one of Lily's many artist friends.

I closed my eyes and inhaled the scent of newness, then opened them, took a hat from the box, and parked it on my head. I modeled it for the tiny back room mirror, turning my head back and forth, nodding it in time to a bop no one could hear.

Someone knocked.

I stopped bopping, stuffed the hat in the box, and pushed the flaps closed. "Yeah?"

"It's me."

Berron.

I set the box on a shelf. "Come in."

He entered and closed the door behind him.

Without warning, I was plunged into the memory of unmasking him as the Prince of the Gentry—trapping him against the wall, pressing my lips to his, discovering a whole new kind of magic as the bright glory of green and gold opened my eyes to his true identity.

"I thought you might need some help," he said.

I cleared my throat. "Help? No help. I'm okay." Very smooth, Zelda.

"What's in the box?"

How did he know? Damn his quiet observance. "A surprise," I said.

"I love surprises," he said.

"Not for you, you selfish thing. For everyone."

"I like everyone surprises. Can I see?"

"You'll see when everyone else sees."

"Come on. Just a peek." He tried puppy-dog eyes on me. Coming from a six-foot-something Gentry prince and not a miniature poodle, it was definitely an odd look. "Please?"

"Fine." I opened the box again and held it out.

His elegant fingers caressed the hat I'd just worn. "Oh," he said, reverently. "Oh, these are *very* nice. Is this… is this for me? To wear?"

I nodded, playing it cool but secretly pleased he was so excited.

He lifted the hat and lowered it onto his head slowly, like he was crowning himself. He turned to the mirror to admire himself. "How do I look? Do I look official?"

"You look like a dork. Not in an ironic, Brooklyn hipster way, but like a regular Joe off the street."

He beamed. "I look normal!"

"You look…"—my tongue suddenly tripped on the words that nearly came out of my mouth: *You look like my ride-or-die*—"really nice," I finished.

The cowardly chicken sounds were so loud in my own mind I was surprised they didn't bring everyone in the restaurant running to find out why I kept live poultry in the back.

Ride-or-die. An expression that meant handing someone your shining golden heart and asking them to kindly not smash it.

I didn't know if I was ready for that—but there would be time to figure that out.

"I think dessert's ready," I said. I dropped my hat back in the box, then took Berron's, too, so as not to ruin the surprise just by walking out.

Berron opened the door and held it for me. I marched out carrying the box, Berron behind me. "Listen up, people. I am about to grant you access to one of the most sought-after artifacts in the known world." I dropped the box on a table with a thump, then beat it like a drumroll.

Everyone quieted.

"Behold," I said. "The official West Side Sandwiches hats!" I whipped two hats out and raised them triumphantly.

"Oh, my!" Poppy said. She hopped out of her chair and hurried forward.

I grinned and handed her one, then tossed the rest like hot dogs at a ball game. Everyone gamely put them on, except Victorine and Jessica. Victorine examined hers like it was an antique medical device: interesting but slightly distasteful. Jessica muttered, "I'm not wearing this," and returned to the kitchen.

"How do I look?" Mom said, preening and patting her exposed hair.

"Marvelous," Victorine said.

"Don't you want to put yours on?"

"Oh, but I must keep it in mint condition," Victorine replied.

The hat suited Daniel fine. Made him look even more like a real New Yorker. Lily, of course, could easily rock a hat. James, too. Even Poppy looked pretty sporty. The Princess of Arrows, on the other hand... let's just say that gold robes and black ball caps are an unusual combo. She didn't seem to be fazed, however, and beamed at everyone like a benevolent sun goddess.

"Too bad they don't make dog hats," I said to Jester. Jester tilted his head to one side, then changed position as if he was considering making a jump for my hat. "Don't even think about it," I told him.

Jessica approached carrying plated cake slices, but I intercepted her. "You're sure you followed the gluten-free procedures?" I said.

"Of course I did. I'm a vampire, not a *monster*," she said. Then she marched past and gave the first slice to Lily, quietly explaining the measures she'd taken to prevent gluten cross-contact.

Pride burst like fireworks.

I took a seat and dug my fork into the deep end of the cake slice, making sure to get lots of frosting, and then hit something green and squishy. I fished out a green candy worm: the proverbial worm in the apple cake. I shook my head and chuckled.

For now, everyone was here—and everything was going to be fine.

18

On the morning of the reverse Manhattanhenge, I woke in the dark before dawn. Mom's early flight gave us just enough time to cruise west to east, facing the rising sun, for the best view of the solar event before turning around and heading out through the Lincoln Tunnel toward New Jersey and the Newark airport.

I wanted her gone, but I wanted her to stay. Relief seasoned with regret. When would we do this again?

Poppy and Berron were the only ones I could convince to come along. Everyone else wanted their beauty sleep. Even Jester didn't bother to get out of his plush dog bed when I hauled myself up. He just lifted his head, blinked sleepily, and then followed me with only his eyes as I got ready.

Downstairs, Poppy—not an early morning person—drank from an oversized coffee mug.

Mom's suitcase sat by the door, as if it was patiently waiting for the rest of us to get it together.

"Where's Mom?" I said.

Poppy gestured toward the door. "Walking with Berron."

"Walking? In the dark?" I went to the window and peered out. In a city that was never truly dark unless the power went out, the street lights cast pools of glowing gold on the pavement. "Why?"

Poppy shrugged and absentmindedly patted her hair, which was still sticking out in all directions. "Perhaps they found an interest in common."

"What would that be?"

"You, obviously."

I went to the coffee machine and poured my own, refusing to look at Poppy.

"You're secretly pleased they get along," Poppy said.

I drank even though the black coffee was too hot and burned my mouth.

"You need to talk to him."

"About what?"

She gave me a look. Wrapped in a thick, pink robe, with her hair in disarray, it was like being pointedly stared at by a giant ruffly-feathered bird. "About your *feelings*."

"What feelings?" I scoffed.

Sweat pinpricked on the back of my neck.

"Oh, I know you tell everyone you're too tough for *feelings*." She launched into an imitation of my voice. "'Men are like Oreos,' you say, 'They're good, but you can't plan your life around them'—"

"Hey, now—"

"But somewhere in that sandwich-padded vault known as your heart, there's a picture of his face right next to Jester's."

"It's too early in the morning to get mushy," I said.

"Lie to yourself if you want," she said, lifting the mug and taking another sip. "But if I had a chance like that, I'd take it. Even if I was afraid it would break my heart in the long run."

A key hit the front door lock, loud in the relative quiet of early morning.

Mom and Berron came through the door all smiles, bundled up in warm clothing against the autumn cold.

"Where've you two been?" I said.

"Berron wanted to show me Central Park in the early morning," Mom said, patting his arm.

"I thought it wasn't open till six."

"No one noticed us," Berron said.

"Funny how that works," I said. "Mom, you ready?"

Mom bustled around, making sure she had everything, and also straightening the couch pillows one last time. "I'm ready!"

Poppy went upstairs to get dressed, then joined us again, looking more awake but not quite fully awake. She yawned. "Let's go see the rising sun thingy."

We went outside, where our breath steamed into the dark. I unlocked Victorine's behemoth black SUV and everyone climbed in: Mom in the front, Poppy and Berron in the passenger row; Berron to the outside since he'd have to be dropped off before we left Manhattan for New Jersey.

I'd read that the best view of the reverse Manhattanhenge was on 41st Street at 5th Avenue, so the plan was to cruise around for a few minutes, then turn east on 41st in time to catch the sun rising in perfect alignment with the city grid. We'd ride down 41st toward the East River, then double back, dropping Berron near the Hudson River walking path. Then we'd take the Lincoln Tunnel over to New Jersey and see Mom safely off on her flight.

Watching the dashboard clock, I took us around Central Park first, past Strawberry Fields and up to the North Woods. We passed Victorine's street and the street for the LWW while going south through the Upper East Side.

The sky began to color.

The timing was right. I continued south on 5th Avenue. We reached the New York Public Library, which faced 41st Street.

"Goodbye, Patience and Fortitude!" Mom waved at the stone library lions. "See you soon!"

We made the turn.

The sun burst into brightness above the edge of the city horizon, a blinding orange slice sliding between the far buildings.

"Ooh," Poppy said. "Very majestic."

It was beautiful—but my stomach did an uncomfortable flip, and my ears felt as if a sudden change in air pressure had occurred.

"Zelda, you okay?" Berron asked.

"Fine," I said, wanting to enjoy the rare sight but also wanting to turn down the next crossing and stop looking at it altogether. I didn't make sense even to myself.

When we finally reached the end of 41st and had to turn north, past the United Nations building, I tried to breathe in relief. Instead, my breath caught like I had a stitch, and as we doubled back to head for the Lincoln Tunnel, I felt like the sun, in the rear-view mirror, was actually crawling up my scalp.

It was so distracting I hit the brakes too hard at a stoplight, throwing everyone forward. "Sorry!" I said. I took my hands off the wheel and shook them out. Get it together, Zelda. "Where do you want me to drop you?" I asked Berron.

"Anywhere after 10th Avenue. I'll walk from there," he said.

The rise in traffic noise felt too much. Too loud. The rising sun too bright. Was this what a migraine felt like? I'd never had one before.

The SUV glided through the city blocks. When we passed 10th Avenue, I pulled over.

Berron jumped out and turned back. "Have a safe flight. I hope we get to see you again soon."

Traffic stopped behind us and cars began to honk enthusiastically.

Mom threw open her door and grabbed Berron in an impromptu hug. "It was wonderful to meet you."

"Mom, we have to go—"

"All right, all right, Zelda, don't get your underwear in a twist." She got back in and waved cheerfully out the window.

Berron grinned and waved back.

We pulled away and quickly outdistanced Berron, even with his long stride.

I joined the arteries of traffic that fed into the Lincoln Tunnel. As we crept forward, walls of brick rose on both sides of the road.

Although the tunnel was lit on the inside, from the outside it looked like a black hole. Police cars were stationed on either side of the final approach.

"Do tunnels bother you?" Poppy asked.

"Bother me?"

"You know—the small space, all that repetitive white tile. The feeling of the whole city pressing down on your head, and then all that water once you're actually underneath the Hudson..."

"No, tunnels *didn't* bother me. Not until you decided to help me out with a really unpleasant description."

"Oops! Sorry," Poppy said.

The car entered the tunnel. Natural morning light gave way to sickly, eye-searing fluorescence. White tile whipped by. The buildings overhead pressed down; we had only a short distance before the tunnel began the actual river crossing.

I'd be fine once we were out in the air again.

I glanced over at Mom.

Mom looked... green. The fluorescent lights?

"Mom, are you okay?" She had that look on her face, the one you never want to see on the face of an aging parent: trying to look stoic for the sake of your kid, even if your kid is a grown adult. "Mom? Talk to me."

Her small form was slipping down in the plush passenger's seat. "I don't feel very well..." Her head rolled unsteadily from side to side, like she couldn't hold it up.

"Poppy, I think something's wrong with—"

But Poppy cried out and clutched her head.

"Poppy?"

Mom's head dropped to her shoulder. Her eyes closed.

"Mom!"

Poppy slumped to the side, her seatbelt stretching as she crumpled sideways onto the bench.

I took one hand off the wheel and shook Mom by the shoulder. "Mom, wake up! Mom!" I turned and grabbed Poppy's knee. "Poppy!"

I needed to turn the car around. I needed to get help. But the tunnel traffic was one way and there was absolutely no way to stop or turn.

Trapped. No way out but through.

My teeth ground against each other as I rode the bumper of the car in front of me.

Had going into the tunnel somehow made both of them sick? Were they food-poisoned? Why not me? What was happening?

"Berron," I said, fumbling for my phone one-handed, dialing. "Come on, pick up." One eye on the road, one eye on my mother and Poppy, stricken in their seats.

"Yeah?" Berron said. His voice crackled and sounded far away. Hopefully the signal boosters in the tunnel would keep us connected.

"Something's happened to Mom and Poppy. We were driving into the tunnel and everything was fine, but then Mom looked sick and Poppy cried out and now they're unconscious and I can't even turn around in this godforsaken tunnel!"

"Unconscious? Like passed out?"

"Yes!"

"Where did it happen?"

"In the tunnel!"

"No—*where* in the tunnel? How far?"

"I don't know, not far? Why does that—"

Not far into the tunnel.

Not far to the river.

To the barrier, which kept the Gentry and the Blessed from leaving the island of Manhattan—and now my mother, and my friend.

"It's the barrier," I said. "It was when we hit the river. They both dropped like sacks of potatoes." I shook Mom again. No good. "Why is this happening? Are they hurt?"

"They'll be okay, I promise. Others have tried to escape over the years—it didn't work, but they weren't permanently harmed by it."

"You never told me that!"

"You never asked!"

"What do I do?"

"Keep driving. The tunnel's only a minute or two more. Then you can exit and turn around. They should be fine once you cross over again. Maybe a little dizzy."

"Like your sister? In Battery Park?"

"Yes."

Looking at my helpless passengers made me want to lower my window and throw up. Instead, I gripped the steering wheel harder.

"Zelda?"

"Yeah?"

"I'll be waiting for you at the tunnel exit."

I couldn't say anything, only blink hard to clear my eyes.

"Do you want me to hang up and let you drive?"

"No, just—" I swallowed. Even Berron's reassurance couldn't stop the horror of seeing Mom and Poppy unresponsive. "Stay with me. Please."

"I'm here. I'm running. I'll be right there when you're out."

More white tile. More hospital fluorescent light. Then, in the distance—a faint orange glow.

The arch of the tunnel exit.

The cars ahead of me sped up.

"Come on, New Jersey," I said, mashing the accelerator.

Never thought I'd be happy to see New Jersey. Brick walls and exposed stone to my right. Industrial buildings to my left. Open sky above, rapidly brightening. Following the signs, trying to picture the swirl of highways that would take me fastest around and back into the tunnel, back to Manhattan. Exiting through another short tunnel, back into daylight. New Jersey proper, with rocky hillsides and apartments and office buildings.

One U-turn and I'd be eastbound.

Done. Then we were flashing past colorful paintings under an overpass. And finally—finally!—a triple archway into the tunnel.

We were in.

"I'm coming," I said to Berron.

"Already there," he said.

Mom's head rolled. I tried to steady her, but there was no fighting the motion of the car. I glanced back at Poppy, who was sprawled out like an overgrown child on a long road trip.

More white tile. I hated the sight of it. I wanted to lean on the horn and go faster, faster, shoot out of that tunnel like a ball from a pinball chute. Thank God it was still early and the traffic hadn't jammed.

Just when it seemed the tunnel might go on forever, possibly under Manhattan and then under the Atlantic Ocean itself, all the way to Poppy's birthplace, the rising sun glared in the distance.

Mom stirred.

The last yards flew by and we were *out*. Back in Manhattan with its glorious congestion and scaffolding.

"I'm almost to you," I said to Berron.

I didn't realize how hard I was shaking until I tried to pull the SUV into the right lane. "Mom? Wake up, we're here." I sounded like the parent. "We're back. Can you hear me?"

Poppy groaned in the back seat. "What in the bloody *hell*...?"

"It's okay," I said, "you're all right. You passed out but you're all right. We're back in Manhattan."

"Zelda?" Mom said, weakly.

"I'm right here, Mom."

She touched a hand to her forehead. "Is this the airport?"

"You got dizzy and we had to come back. Do you feel okay?"

"I feel like my head's full of bees."

"What happened?" Poppy said. "Why did we—"

"The barrier," I said.

"But *why*?"

"I don't know." I spotted Berron and pulled over.

He pulled open the passenger door and slid into the third row, leaving Poppy her space to recover. "You ladies scared me," he said, leaning over to peer at Poppy and Mom in turn. "Do we need a hospital? I think the nearest one is—"

"I don't need a hospital, I need an airplane," Mom said.

"Mom, you passed out. I'm not putting you on a plane."

"I'll be *fine*. I got a little dizzy, that's all."

"You *can't* leave—that's what I'm trying to tell you. If I take you back through that tunnel, you'll pass out all over again."

"Why would it happen again?"

"You know how I told you that the Gentry and the Blessed can't leave Manhattan? Because of the spell Grandma helped put in place to keep the peace?"

"Yes..."

I shrugged, as if to say, *there you have it.*

"But I don't want to stay in New York! I want to go *home*, Zelda. No offense," she added, politeness coming back online as she became more and more with it.

"You can't. Not now. Not until we figure out what's going on."

"Oh, no," Poppy said. In the rear-view mirror, her eyes widened. "What if it wasn't just us?"

"What do you mean?"

"What if it's *all* the witches?"

Everyone got quiet. I pictured witches on trains, buses; in taxis; passing out with no one to ferry them back. Or, God forbid, what if they were *driving*? "Get ahold of Azure," I said. "Start a phone chain or something."

Poppy pulled out her phone and began frantically texting.

Meanwhile, my mother was muttering to herself. "Can't stay here. Even the sunrise isn't normal."

"What are you talking about?"

"Well, just look at it! You said it's supposed to be in perfect alignment with the street grid. But there it is, drifting off to the north!"

I slowed to a stop at the next light. "No, it's still in alignment, we're just coming at it from a different angle because we're not on the same street."

"Not there," Mom said. She leaned over and pointed toward the driver's side window. "*There.*"

I turned. Saw a *second* orange-gold glow.

And the *too bright, too loud*, came back with a vengeance, honking horns hitting my eyes with waves of pain. Everything jangled—the sound of traffic, the sunlight hitting the Midtown windows—until suddenly the jangling resolved into something lighter, harmonic, musical.

Bells.

19

I squeezed my eyes shut. Afterimages burst behind my eyelids. I opened my eyes and glanced at Mom, who was squinting out the window. "Mom, don't stare at the sun."

It wasn't the sun. I knew it wasn't, even as I jammed the accelerator down and Victorine's SUV lunged through the intersection.

"Zelda," Berron said.

"What?" I snapped. The barrier had gone haywire, Mom couldn't leave, and now I was trying to pilot this behemoth through what was rapidly turning into rush hour.

"It's coming closer."

"Oh, no..." Poppy said, as she pressed against the window for a better view.

"What?" I nearly yelled. "What's 'Oh, no'?"

I didn't need to ask. I just didn't want to see.

The light turned green and horns blared behind us. I made them wait.

I made myself look.

Golden robes crackling with magic like electricity. Golden hair, floating unnaturally; locks curling in and out at the tips like octopus arms. And a face I never wanted to see again, turning toward me with glowing eyes. Smiling. A beautiful smile, on molten glass lips.

The Arcade.

I could have kept driving. I could have gotten out and walked. Over a bridge, through a tunnel; far, far away. Fat lot of good it would have done—it didn't matter if *I* could get off this island, because none of the people I cared for could come with me.

"Berron. Poppy," I said. "I'm going to drop you off. Take Mom home and keep her safe. I'm going after this... *thing*."

"Zelda Hawkins, you will do no such thing," Mom said.

"Mom, you are not getting involved in this."

"Try getting me out of this car," she said. "Just try. You won't have any eyebrows left."

I squeezed the steering wheel. "*Please.*"

"No."

"It looks like it's coming up 40th," Poppy said. "Or maybe 41st. I can't tell."

"That's the Manhattanhenge alignment," I said, turning down an avenue. Skyscrapers made the Arcade disappear, and for a few moments, I could imagine that everything was normal—until I made another turn and saw the Arcade floating over the New York Public Library, high in the air above the two famous lions. "What's she doing?"

"Nothing good," Berron said.

"Oh, you *think*?"

"What are those silver swirly things?" Mom said.

"What silver swirly things?" Then I saw them: fine threads of silver wrapping themselves around her, turning gold.

"That's magic," Poppy said. "She's... absorbing it?"

"From where?" Mom said.

"New York," Berron said. "Like the Forest of Emeralds."

"Not if I can help it," I said.

"She's floating in the sky," Poppy said. "How are we going to reach her?"

Everyone fell silent. Out of nowhere, I pictured the glider from *Escape from New York*, the movie Daniel and I had watched on my first night in the city. A glider that had landed on a rooftop.

A rooftop!

"Daniel's condo," I said. "It overlooks Bryant Park. The building has a garden on the roof."

"He still has that condo?" Poppy said.

"You still have a key?" Berron added.

I looked in the rearview. Mischief glinted in his eyes, even at a time like this. "Stop wiggling your eyebrows at me and help me find a place to ditch this car." Victorine was going to murder me if it was impounded, but that paled in comparison to whatever the Arcade was up to.

Luckily, we found a spot around the corner. Everyone got out.

"Mom," I said, giving it one last try. "Let me get you a cab home."

She pointed to the Arcade, who continued to hoover up silver wisps of magic. "You want me to toddle off while you face this alone? Stop wasting time." She whirled, marched off, then stopped. "Which one is Daniel's building?"

I pointed the opposite direction from where she'd been heading. She huffed and walked off.

I managed to catch up and lead the way, Berron and Poppy following, all of us dodging the office-suited people on their way to their normal, office jobs.

When we went through the building doors, warm air rushed out—the exact opposite of the first time I'd walked through them at the height of summer, when the air conditioning had nearly frozen my sweat.

Although the doorman didn't know me by sight, the key card I waved kept him from taking too much interest.

We entered the elevator. I pushed the button, the doors slid closed, and we surged upward until my ears popped, passing Daniel's old floor.

At the top floor, the bell dinged, and I jumped like the Arcade was right behind me. I took a breath and walked out of the elevator.

The hallway was noticeably cooler than the lobby, as if the building didn't bother to pump the heat this high. Floor-to-ceiling windows revealed a view of outdoor couches and tables arranged on artificial turf. It would have been peaceful if I didn't know what was floating nearby.

I put my hand on the door to the outside.

"Wait," Poppy said. "What's the plan?"

"The plan?" I said. "Mom'll burn the Arcade's eyebrows off. Right, Mom?"

"Right," she said, looking small but particularly fierce.

I pushed the door open.

Cold air barrelled across the patio; the higher the altitude, the higher the wind speed. My hat blew off but I caught it in-flight and shoved it into my pocket.

We crossed the artificial turf and approached the lookout over Bryant Park and 41st Street.

Below, the everyday city business: people rushing, cars stopping and going, the smell of breakfast food trucks and exhaust rising as high as a skyscraper.

And, hovering above where 41st ran into the New York Public Library, my old enemy.

The Arcade.

She floated in what looked like serene contemplation, a meditative goddess, almost peaceful—benevolent-looking, even—until you saw the silver magic drawn from below, wrapping around her tentacle hair like old-fashioned curl papers, and then, with one last bright flash of defiance, becoming absorbed into the gold.

"She's getting stronger," Berron said.

"How are we supposed to fight it?" Mom said. "She's over there. And, well"—she gestured to the fake green grass we stood on—"we're over here."

Mom was right. The last time I'd fought the Arcade, she'd been careless enough to let us get close.

"She doesn't look particularly concerned," Poppy added.

The silver magic fled the city faster, as if her appetite was growing.

"She's showing off," I said.

"What happens if she sucks it all up?" Mom said.

"Nothing good."

"We can't just stand here." Mom wound up like she was going to throw a baseball, then chucked a ball of fire into the air in the direction of the Arcade.

The fireball burned itself out a few dozen feet from Daniel's building.

"Mom! You can't just—chuck fireballs off a building!"

"You got a better idea?"

Manhattanhenge, still aligned with the city grid, bore down on all of us, painting the Arcade inferno orange.

Poppy tried next, launching a respectable fireball that again fell far short of the target. She leaned over as if winded. "Why do I feel so *knackered*?"

"If she's sucking up all the magic, it's not as easy for you to access it," I said. "And the longer we stand here, the worse it will get." I pulled off my gloves and conjured fire in my cupped hands by thinking of hot kitchen things: ovens, griddles, elements. The flames sprang to life and inflated to beach ball size. I lifted the fireball and hurled it in the direction of the Arcade.

It soared, then winked out short of the target. Farther than Mom's, but shorter than Poppy's.

"Damn it," I said.

"What if the three of you worked together?" Berron said. "Pool your fire magic."

Mom, Poppy, and I looked at each other. What was there to lose?

"Come on." I held my bare hand palm-up. "It's worth a shot."

"What do we do?" Mom said.

"Imagine you're fueling a fire. Same thing you do as when you prepare to throw a fireball, only you're going to concentrate on aiming it right here." I moved my hand up and down like I was weighing a ball of dough. "I'll pull the magic away from you and throw it. Got it?"

Mom nodded.

Their magic poured into my hand. It swirled around and around as if that ball of dough had been thrown into a mixer on high speed. Following the pattern of its spin, I waited until it glowed so brightly silver I could hardly look at it—then I launched it.

The silver cannonball flew high, arcing even higher than we stood on top of the building, before tumbling downward and burning out short of the Arcade.

We missed.

But we'd drawn her attention.

Her head turned until her glowing eyes had us in their sights. Though I should have been blinded by them, like headlights, instead darkness descended, like she'd swallowed Manhattanhenge along with the magic.

In the dark place, came her voice.

Zelda. I have finished the work your grandmother's generation began. The barrier is sealed at last. I will take all the magic, until there is none left; until everything is peaceful.

As you always wished it to be.

"I never asked for that!"

Did you not? The Arcade's expression could have been carved ice. *And when I am finished, I will pull the Forest of Emeralds up by its roots and have its magic as well. You will be helpless. You will be, at long last...*

Normal.

The word sliced through me like a jagged cut from a dull knife. Truth brought shame. I *had* wished for normal, once upon a time.

But that time had passed, and I wasn't that Zelda anymore.

"I am not *normal!*" Anger sent tremors through my body. I seized my mother's hand, then Poppy's. "And neither are they! And that's..." I looked at Mom. "That's *okay*. We don't have to be normal." I felt Berron behind me, then, placing his hands on my shoulders. Supporting me.

My mother; my friend; my... Berron. I had things to say to him, when this was done.

You will not stop me, the Arcade said. *You are weak.*

"Not being 'normal,'" I said, "is our *strength*." My hands sparkled, as they often did after I had petted Jester, since that day at the charity auction when he ate the four-leaf clovers.

Take me down and the barrier falls with me. You will destroy what your grandmother helped build.

Was I destroying my grandmother's legacy? The shop still stood. My memories burned bright. Grandma protected New York the best way she knew how. So did I.

Was this destruction—or was it evolution?

I saw the faces of those I loved most, and I knew the answer.

"Let it fall," I said. "It's time to try something new."

I squeezed Mom and Poppy's hands. *Fire*, I thought. *Fire* and *flight. Fire* and *soaring over the city fueled by magic and the sun—*

And love.

Love for the magic of New York. Of my mother and my grandmother. Of the witches, the Gentry, and the Blessed.

The world was growing dark, but we were a beacon; we shone; we gathered to ourselves everything the Arcade could never take, never understand.

My chest hurt. I had never given birth, but some primitive part of me knew that something was coming.

A new creature, born of flames.

Wings, unfolding in silver cascades, beating in slow motion like the chambers of my heart. A head adorned with delicate curling feathers. A pointed beak. Eagle-like claws. A body as gracefully shaped as an expensive vase in the Met.

A phoenix!

None of us had ever manifested a true familiar—but together, we had created something even greater and more beautiful than any familiar I'd ever seen.

The bird rose, trailing sparks. It flapped its wings, setting a course for the Arcade.

The wind from its wings blew hot against us, whipping the cold air to make whirlwinds that sent the pillows tumbling off the couches and across the turf.

But the firebird hung in mid-air—not retreating, not getting closer to the Arcade.

"Why isn't it moving?" I said.

"Magic can only go so far," Poppy said. "It has to burn something to keep going."

"What can it burn?" Mom said. "It's in the sky!"

"And if it sets anything on fire," I said, looking at Bryant Park, the library, the surrounding buildings, "someone could get hurt."

Berron's hands left my shoulders.

He moved to the edge of the patio.

He turned back. Looked at me. Smiled. His ears regained their natural points. His modern clothes turned fairy-in-the-forest, rich and brown and not of this Earth, piped with gold—except for the West Side Sandwiches hat, the perfect accessory for any outfit. "Tell my sister," he said, "that I love her."

My heart skipped, and the phoenix lost a little altitude. "Berron," I said, "what are you doing?"

"And tell yourself," he continued, as if I hadn't spoken, "the same. Except very, very different." He doffed the cap, like a gentleman, then tugged it back in place and turned away.

Before I could let the phoenix evaporate like fog in the sun, consequences be damned, he climbed onto the ledge.

Unbidden, the words of the book I found in Prospero's apartment, *Manners for Men*, came back to me.

Reliable as rocks...

His clothes roughened like bark, then his skin; fingers lengthened into branches and twigs; feet became roots that gripped the side of the building.

Judicious in every action...

And then the tree that was Berron grew and grew, reaching across the space between our building and the next, suspended in space across two root systems, a canopy exploding open like an umbrella, reaching for the phoenix.

Dependable in trifles as well as the large affairs of life...

In the space of moments, the prince's tree grew from spring to summer, then burst with autumn apples, and then stood in craggy winter form, dry and stripped of leaves and fruit.

Full of mercy and kindness to others...

A lifeline. A lifeline meant to burn.

His life is pure and kindly.

I realized I was screaming when my throat hurt. My fire mouse burst from me and ran for the roots, tiny frantic squeaks lost in the crackle of leaves and branches growing toward destruction.

"Berron, no..." But it barely came out. My voice was gone.

The phoenix landed in the tree and the whole city seemed to inhale. The phoenix expanded, brightened, took on the color of true fire, not just silver magic, as it incinerated the tree from its crown to the smallest tendril of its roots. Ash rained down as the phoenix took flight once more, a flaming arrow aimed at the heart of the Arcade.

She turned. Her hair curled up at the tips in rage. Her eyes beamed hatred; I felt it through Mom and Poppy, too, each of us conducting power like the wires of the city itself, competing with the pull of the Arcade.

The phoenix bent its wings and plunged.

Fueled by magic, roaring with fire, the phoenix struck the Arcade full in the chest. Gold and silver and orange exploded as if the Manhattanhenge sun had fallen to earth and cracked in half like an egg.

A sound of breaking glass; of bells that would never ring again.

Stolen magic billowed free.

The city exhaled.

When the smoke cleared, the phoenix remained. It banked over the stone lions and let out a call, triumphant and musical but also a little bit like the faraway horns of morning traffic. It was a New York bird, after all. Then it glided back and landed on the edge of the roof.

The Arcade, gone. The great split-rooted, building-spanning tree, gone.

Berron, gone.

Just Mom, Poppy, me, and a phoenix. It preened its feathers and small embers fell out, scorching the fake turf.

My cheeks were cold. Wet. I let go of Mom and Poppy's hands and approached the phoenix. Radiant warmth dried my cheeks, the salt pulling the skin tighter.

I reached a hand out, gently. Could you pet a phoenix? It had always worked for Jester. I touched the bird's head and smoothed back the curly feathers.

The bird looked at me gravely. Then it stuck its neck out and pecked at my hat.

"I think it wants it," Mom said. "Your hat."

I scrubbed at my stinging eyes. "Why do you want my hat?" I said.

It cocked its head impatiently.

I thought of Berron wearing his hat, staring at himself in the mirror and being so pleased, and my stomach lurched. I took the hat off. "Here."

The bird seized it in its beak. It looked around—at Poppy, at Mom, at me. At the sun. Then it flapped its wings and soared away, its reflection glinting in the windows of the surrounding buildings, finally dissolving into the bright sky over Bryant Park.

Hat and all.

20

Berron was gone.

In the month that passed since the Arcade fell, my mother stayed in town and ran the restaurant until I could be trusted not to fry my tears on the griddle, or wield my chef's knife so hard I nearly split a cutting board.

The Princess traded her gold robes for white, and led her people in strange rituals I didn't understand but participated in all the same.

Berron couldn't help me hide the unseasonable greenery anymore; it fell to me, and the Princess, to walk the streets and make the magic sleep as it should. In the gray and the snow of New York, she was a sad but beautiful vision, almost ghostlike.

Jester wore his little jacket and tiny snow boots. The sight of him in his winter gear was the only thing that kept my heart from turning to ice.

The Princess didn't say much.

Neither did I.

When our task was done, she ushered me back to the hidden portal in Gramercy Park. Jester's leash tangled briefly in the leaves. The ice-coated branches stung when they hit my cheeks—or they would have, if my cheeks weren't already numb.

Numb, as I had learned, is a haven. A refuge.

And a hell.

When the worst happened, when it was so new I leaned on Poppy for comfort, she saw it all. I had to pull away because I couldn't stand to put her through the howling abyss in my head.

She understood. She was too kind not to, and that made my self-imposed withdrawal hurt even more.

They were too good to me. All of them. My mother, benevolently bossing everyone around. Poppy, walking the dogs when my body was too heavy to drag out of bed. Daniel, rolling up his sleeves and pitching in at West Side Sandwiches. James, making sure to shove a plate of food at me; and Jessica, needling me until I gave in and ate. Victorine, sitting beside me in silence, because sometimes that's all you can do.

And Jester, of course, whose doggy life went on as usual but for the strange times he would look out the window as if expecting someone familiar to arrive; or when he flung himself heavily across my lap and looked at me with dark, wise eyes.

I stepped into the Forest of Emeralds. Ice crunched in the grass underfoot. The weather reflected the season, or the Princess of Arrows's mood, or both. Dead leaves dropped like confetti at a funeral. Another reminder that this was Berron's true home; that he was a prince; that I'd lost him—and it was all my fault.

"It was not your fault," the Princess of Arrows said, reading my face as easily as Poppy read minds.

I was too polite to argue. But if I let her try to soothe me, I would hate myself. She lost her brother, after all. I lost… a friend? Because I was too much of a coward to let it be anything more?

I hated myself anyway.

We walked on in silence, a strange bird calling out overhead, unseen. Jester romped and sniffed, tugging me to move faster along the path.

After we passed through the apple orchard and reached the Fortress of Apples, the Princess stopped. "May I offer you a hot drink?"

The stone doors on the lowest level of the Fortress wrapped around out of sight. One of them was Berron's, where he'd offered us tea and had a rousing argument with Daniel. I squeezed my eyes shut, then blinked furiously. "I'm good. Thanks."

"Do you wish me to accompany you?"

She always asked.

"No," I said. I always declined. "Thank you, though."

"As you wish." She laid her hand on my arm, her white bell sleeve shimmering with silver threads. "I miss him, too."

I nodded, not trusting myself to speak, wondering when it would become less hard.

She let me go.

I turned toward the path that led to the Vale of Amethysts, where they had all gone that day I was too busy to stay and journey with them.

The forest opened up to a rock formation with a narrow opening in the middle, just big enough for a person to slip through. Plenty of space for a mini poodle.

How many times had I replayed what I had missed that day? Berron, my mother, Poppy, and the Princess squeezing through the gap, their laughter echoing. Jester dashing ahead. Emerging breathless on the other side, to see...

This:

A trail paved with tiny crystals shading from purple to white to clear. Scoop up a handful and they sparkle in the sun. The amethyst cliffs and boulders look slick, are slick, but what looks like wetness is in fact a gemstone's reflection, so dark it could be black, until the light hits it and it glows purple from the inside.

Little wildflowers all around, white and purple as if planted on purpose to match. Green vines, twin to the ones in Gramercy Park, climbing over and around everything.

The whole place smelled like minerals and candied pansies; like a flower-strewn cake on a slate platter.

Jester surged forward so hard I stumbled and kicked up a hail of amethysts.

"Hang on, bud!"

He didn't listen. On a downward slope I was helpless to do anything but slip and slide until we reached the lowest point of the valley.

At the bottom, you can look up and see nothing but amethyst walls and sky.

On the right side of the path, a tree split itself over a rock formation. Two great gnarls of roots twisted downward and gripped the amethysts. The trunk rose like a wishbone handle to support sweeping branches covered in brown leaves that rattled in the wind.

Berron took them here. To crunch along the gemstone path. To smell the sugary flowers. To nestle in the roots of the split-root tree and gaze up at the passing clouds, while he handed around odd Gentry snacks and flasks of sapphire-berry juice and floral tea.

I clambered up the rocks and lowered myself into my usual nook in the roots, shifting into a comfortable-enough position.

Jester sniffed the base of the tree with far too much interest.

"Don't even think about it," I said.

He sat down and huffed—a doggy half-sneeze of frustration—before climbing into my lap. His nose twitched at the cold breeze.

I placed one hand on Jester's back, one hand on a tree root, and sighed. He came here to think. To rest. And now, so did I.

"Hey, Berron," I said.

I'd been coming here for a month and I hardly knew why. Of all the places I'd been with Berron—the restaurant, the parks, the Fortress, the orchard, the bar where he drank too much—the place

I came back to was the place I'd never been with him. Maybe it was self-torture for everything I hadn't said or done that I should have.

"It's Christmastime in the city," I continued. "Lights. Holiday foods at the food carts. Everybody suddenly getting into hot cocoa and apple cider even though it's been cold for months." I chuckled to myself. "And now that the barrier is down, the Christmas shopping is out of *hand*. I've never seen so many vampires excited to go to some mall in New Jersey."

I rummaged in my coat pocket. "I did a little shopping myself. Got you something." I pulled out a crinkly vacuum-sealed package of coffee beans from a hipster shop in Brooklyn, then tore open the seal. The scent of coffee overwhelmed the smell of the flowers. I scooped up a handful of roasted beans and scattered them over the roots.

Jester lunged, but when he took an experimental coffee bean lick, he made a face and flopped back on my lap.

"You never got to have that Coney Island vegetarian hot dog," I said, sprinkling more coffee beans, "but I figured it might be kind of messy. Didn't want to mustard your tree." I brushed a few coffee skins off my hands. We had talked, once, about going to Florida, before I knew who and what he truly was. Someday I would bring beach sand back, and add it to the little amethysts at the base of the tree.

"I'm just..." I paused, trying to think of what to say. "I don't know."

There was no one to judge what I said. No one but a poodle, who thought everything I said was genius.

"I miss walking the city with you. It's not the same."

I took a breath, watched it curl out in steam.

Jester looked at me.

"When I came here, all of us wanted *so much*. At first, I didn't know what was genuine, versus what was just another way for someone to get what they wanted. What *I* wanted," I added, knowing I'd done the same.

"I didn't trust anyone, except for Poppy and this stupid dog. And maybe I was right about that. At first." I patted Jester, absently. "I thought... I thought there would be more *time*—" I stopped as my voice seized up.

Jester leaped up and began licking my cheeks.

"Get off, dog," I said, but I was hugging him and he couldn't have left if he wanted to.

I curled up, holding Jester and nestling tightly into the trunk of the tree. "I'm sorry, Berron. I should have told you—"

Even Jester couldn't catch all the teardrops before they hit the tree roots.

"I'm sorry," I whispered, wishing I could have one more chance. One time to start over. One rewind. Go back to that first day in the shop and do it all differently.

Jester wriggled. I didn't want to squish the poor guy, so I let him go. He scratched at the tree roots.

"I said, don't even think about it."

He ignored me and launched into a full, double-pawed, rapid-fire dig.

I wiped my eyes on my sleeve and sat up fully. "Dude. One minute ago, you're kissing my face. Now you're ignoring me to dig up a tree? Not cool." I placed my hand above where he'd been digging.

The wood was *warm*.

"What the..."

Jester whined and pawed at the spot again.

I stood up, found a spot where I could balance between the split roots, and pressed both hands against the tree.

Something like gold sap was *racing* under my fingers.

"What is this?" I said.

It felt like springtime. It felt like life. It felt like laughter. It felt golden and...

Royal.

Goosebumps rose on my arms. I leaned harder on the tree and propped my forehead against the bark. My Gentry magic was on *fire*, and I poured it into the wood like thick pancake batter into a hot frying pan.

Lattices of golden power danced over the trunk. Cascaded over the roots. I lifted my head and looked up—the papery dead leaves were now alive with gold, and dancing in a wind that seemed to be made of magic itself.

Jester barked.

I gripped the tree and pushed harder, my own hands glowing gold and sparkling, too. I looked down, beneath my feet, where the roots plunged below the amethysts.

And then, I saw—

Berron, the Prince of the Gentry.

Asleep, under the roots.

"Berron!" I stared in shock. Hallucination or not, hope surged like a pot boiling over. "Wake up!" I found a coffee bean underfoot and crushed it. "Wake up and smell the coffee!"

The Berron hallucination rolled over.

"Berron! You stupid idiot!" I kicked the tree for good measure. "Wake. Up! I *love* you, dammit!"

A gold explosion blinded me. I fell, landing heavily on my ass with a root in the wrong place. I still had the leash and Jester was barking madly. I blinked against what had become the sun—and not the winter sun, mind you, cold and white, but a blazing spring sun out to settle scores with the snow.

And when it faded, the Prince's Tree shone with new leaves, and *he* stood before me.

Smiling. Pointy-eared. Kind of full of himself. *And still with the West Side Sandwiches hat on his head.*

My mouth fell open. "Where'd you get that?" I said.

"A little birdie gave it to me."

Jester was on two legs jumping up and down like a little man as he tried to get to Berron. I made it easy by stumbling forward, never mind the roots, and hurling myself into Berron's arms.

Jester jumped and snorfed and pawed at the two of us as we held each other.

"I thought you were gone," I said, breathing the scent of his shoulder.

"I thought I was too," he said.

I grabbed him by the hat brim and gave him a little shake. "Don't you ever scare me like that again."

"Why? Will you break up with me?"

"Who said I was dating you?"

He arched an eyebrow.

"All right, fine," I said. "If you have to put a label on it."

He laughed, removed the hat, and swooped in for what would have been very embarrassing kisses down the side of my neck. But since only the dog was watching, they were actually pretty nice. "I love you, too," he said, when he had made it all the way to my collarbone.

"Mm," I said, struck slightly dumb by shock, magic, and more feelings than I had bargained for. "Are we making out now?"

"Yes," he said, straightening up and booping my nose with one long, elegant finger. "So. Where to first? Coney Island? Brooklyn?"

My mind whirled. The whole world, wide open.

Freedom—at last—for all of us.

"It's going to take a little planning," I said, "but we're going on a field trip."

21

The day had arrived, and I stood in Riverside Park and shivered. Normally, walking kept me warm enough under all my winter layers, but Berron said he wanted to surprise me—and to do that, I had to stand in the snow. The 91st Street Garden slept under its snow blanket, only disturbed by Berron's footprints after he disappeared inside.

"Should have asked him to warm me up," I said to myself, remembering his warming magic only a few minutes too late.

Snow had fallen on New York, frosting every branch, covering the ground. The snow had blown in with such wind that it stuck to the windward side of the trees as if it had been carefully sprayed on. The snow lay on top of the old-fashioned lamps like a cap, and on the benches like a cold, custom-fit cushion.

The wind had stopped after the storm, leaving everything crystal and perfect. The parks department had cleared the walkways and stairs, but everything else was uninterrupted white powder.

Anything resembling a slope had kids and adults trying to sled down it.

I bounced up and down on the balls of my feet, trying to stay warm and dispel my impatience.

Then, I heard it—

A crackle of bent branches. A shower of fallen snow. Clip-clops on stone pavers, faster and faster—

And a horse, flying over the 91st Street Garden fence, legs extended, mane flying, and the Prince of the Gentry on her back.

They landed with a thud that shook the ground and sent a spray of snow through the air.

"Showoffs," I said.

Berron bowed from Sybelia's star-scattered back. Sybelia just snorted. "Come on up," Berron said. "The weather's fine."

I took his arm and managed to clamber up in front of him. "At least the horse is warm," I said, taking the reins.

Sybelia, who had a mind of her own, began to walk.

"So am I," Berron said, passing his arms around my waist, his breath warm and tickling my neck.

"Make yourself useful and crank up the heat." I felt him smile without needing to look, and delicious warmth spread over me with tendrils of green and gold magic. "We can't do this for too long. Everyone will be waiting."

"I know," he said. "But how many days do we get like this? The sun will come out, and all of this will melt." He paused. "Do you like my surprise?"

"A horseback ride through a winter wonderland? Worst surprise ever."

He thumped his hand into his chest. "My lady cuts me to the quick! I am deceased, you hear me? Deceased!"

I pulled the reins. "Whoa," I said to Sybelia. I turned and kissed Berron's cheek. "Not on my watch," I said. I turned around and clicked my tongue.

Sybelia danced sideways for a moment before launching into a peppy trot.

Passers-by pointed and waved at the sight of us.

Berron, of course, waved back.

"Stop waving."

"Why?"

"You're acting like royalty."

"I *am* royalty."

"They don't know that."

"On some level they do," Berron said, with confidence so smooth it could have buttered bread.

"So modest."

"One of my many qualities." He gave me a little squeeze, and I couldn't help it—I laughed. "Try it," he added. "You'll like it."

"I'm not waving at people."

"Come on, my Zelda," he said. "Just try it."

It was the *my Zelda* that did it. We were approaching a group of children building a snow-something—the exact shape wasn't quite clear yet—and I tentatively raised a hand.

The kids broke into whoops, and waved back.

"See? Already a queen," Berron said.

"I'm the queen of New York!" I said, getting into it.

We rode on, laughing and talking about nothing much at all. You don't always appreciate those moments of *nothing much* until you've been through the fire. As far as I was concerned, I would be holding each and every one of those *nothing much* moments close like they were the last drops of sapphire-berry juice shaken out of a flamingo-stemmed goblet.

By the time we had ridden out and back, it was time to meet up with the others for our field trip.

Mom had gone safely home—and Lily with her, for a winter family vacation in Florida.

Victorine, the fuddy-duddy, had claimed that one place was much like another, and she would rather stay in her Upper East Side home and tend her orchids.

But Poppy, Daniel, Jessica, James, and the Princess were game.

The Princess of Arrows returned with Berron when he took Sybelia back to the Forest of Emeralds, and the three of us headed for the appointed subway station to meet the rest of the gang.

"I have never ridden this 'subway,'" the Princess of Arrows said, once again resplendent in gold.

What do you say to that? *You're in for a treat*? "It's something," I said.

"I prefer Sybelia," Berron said, "but she doesn't carry seven."

Underground, I scanned the subway platform. "James!" I called.

His black leather duster spun open as he turned. A gray streak in his hair caught the light like ice. He waved.

Since I'd started slowly moving his vampire magic to Jessica, he was the happiest almost-middle-aged man in Manhattan. It required holding hands with both of them for long periods of time, and left me craving steak afterward, but they were both getting what they needed.

Jessica, Daniel, and Poppy joined us.

And we were off, a small crowd moving through the larger one that milled around the subway platform. A breeze kicked up, pushed out of the tunnel by an oncoming train.

"That's ours," I said. "Last one to Battery Park's a rotten egg!"

The train squealed to a stop and the doors sighed open. People made their way off the train and we made our way in, settling into hard plastic seats underneath ads and diagrams of the subway system.

At the last second, two more men jumped on.

With a guitar and an accordion.

The Princess of Arrows clapped her hands in delight. "Musicians!" She looked at the other passengers, who—every single one of them—immediately became fascinated by their phones, a book, or looking in any direction but at the two musicians. "Why do they not show their joy?"

"It overwhelms them," Berron said, obviously trying hard to keep a straight face.

"Ah," the Princess said, nodding. The two subway performers struck up a folk song. The Princess of Arrows rose to her slippered feet and began to delicately soft-shoe.

"Go on, my Berron," I said. "Just try it."

He shot me a look. "Someday," he said, "I will have my revenge." He stood, took his sister's hands, and joined her in the dance.

"That's actually quite catchy," Poppy said. She stood up, gripped a subway pole for balance, and began to boogie side-to-side.

James jumped up and struck a Saturday Night Fever pose.

Jessica shaded her face with one hand. "I don't know any of you."

I was too busy watching the antics to notice that Daniel had glided over. "May I have this dance?" he said. "For old times' sake."

And then we were dancing, too, but laughing too much to do it well. When the next stop came, everyone switched partners, and Daniel dragged Jessica to her feet.

By the time we arrived at Battery Park, we had entertained, confused, or annoyed hundreds of subway passengers.

We disembarked and headed upstairs.

Inside Battery Park, even the SeaGlass Carousel appeared to be covered in powdered sugar. We passed it and continued to the dockside promenade, where we presented our tickets to Statue City Cruises.

From the dock level upward, the three-story ferry was as white as the snow. If I didn't know better, I would have thought it had been sculpted in the park and then set in the harbor. But it was solid and reassuringly steady as we crossed the gangplank and boarded.

"Which level?" I called over my shoulder.

"Top!" cried Poppy.

"It's freezing up there!"

Poppy made jazz hands and wiggled her fingers at me, as if to remind me of her fire magic.

I found the stairs and headed up, past the second level, to the open-aired third level with rows of all-white benches. Unsurprisingly, we had it entirely to ourselves.

When all the passengers had boarded, the ferry engines rumbled.

Poppy was humming to herself—the tune from the subway—and a twinkling silver glitter drifted over all of us.

Toasty warmth surrounded me.

The ferry chugged away from the dock. From the harbor, the skyline looked completely different, as if leaving it changed it completely. When I stood on the city streets, it felt like *my* city. Looking back at it, over the distance and the water, it felt like *everyone's* city.

The Statue of Liberty came into view. Small, as the Princess of Arrows had said, but getting bigger every second.

The arrival dock lay behind the Statue, facing an American flag that waved in the harbor breeze. Snow coated the small stand of trees nearby.

Already we had come so far, past anywhere the Blessed or the Gentry could have gone before. I smiled. Set my cap firmly. Waited for the ferry to dock securely.

Berron was at the railing, his hands gripping the rail until small vines grew, his gaze on the Statue. The second the boat stilled, he was moving for the stairs.

I jumped up and herded the rest of our crew down, to find Berron waiting on the ferry side of the gangplank. "What are you waiting for?" I said.

"You."

A whole world inside one word.

Our slow and careful walk down the gangplank turned reckless when we reached dry, solid ground. Poppy and the Princess of Arrows galloped at full tilt over the brick promenade. Berron, Daniel, and James jostled each other good-naturedly, like boys, while Jessica, like a dark horse, sprinted ahead of all of us, arms pumping, head held high. James dropped back with a good-natured laugh and waved them on, his human side beginning to show in gasps for air.

When the brick path narrowed and began to curve around the star-shaped stone fort, we all slowed and walked together.

When we reached our destination, and gazed upward together, no one spoke.

Beyond the roof of the fort, above the stone pedestal with its edges piped with snow, stood the Statue of Liberty. Her arm, well-muscled like a baker's; her crown, a halo and a pointed defense against those who would challenge her. She was strong—for us.

We would be strong for each other.

I thought of my grandmother: sandwiches, bowls of fluffy potato salad, cold glasses of milk and pans of apple tarts overflowing with cinnamon and sugar. Summer mornings on the Central Park lawn. Letting the magic in.

Setting the magic free.

The Statue stared out at the harbor, holding her torch with the golden flame. Watching the ships come in, watching the seasons change.

Until the clouds shifted, and the shadows played over her face; and it seemed, for only a few breaths, that she turned her gaze on us.

And she smiled.

Epilogue

Nothing tests a relationship like a sixteen-hour drive. Especially when you add in a nervous mini poodle and a co-pilot with a brand new driver's license.

Jester eventually stopped shaking in his doggy safety harness, but I couldn't say the same for myself—not when Berron was at the wheel.

Berron quoted obscure road rules for fun, then ignored them completely and lead-footed it to every possible side trip, tourist trap, and u-pick fruit farm.

I, on the other hand, viewed the expanse between New York and Florida as something to be passed through as quickly as possible.

It made for an interesting road trip.

When we finally broke the Florida state line and blew south on I-95, the humidity wrapped me up like one of Grandma's quilts. It wasn't summer yet, only spring break, and the heat was strong but tolerable.

The exit to Sparkle Beach took us through town: past landmarks like the old Highway to Grill burger joint; cruising the River Street downtown district; and finally over a great, swooping arch of a bridge above the Intercoastal Waterway to the beachside peninsula, where my cousin Luella lived.

We wouldn't be staying in her cozy shotgun shack, though. Lily claimed that spare bedroom, so we had our own digs at the Eventide Motel, adjacent to Rolling Wave Coffee. Word was that the coffee there rivaled even that of the Big Apple.

But since we were running a little behind schedule—one "Let's check out where that road goes!" too many—we were heading straight for the beach.

The rental car crunched over shell-peppered sand in the beachside parking lot just as the sun began to slide past the western horizon. The condo buildings and palm trees cast long shadows.

Berron was practically bouncing up and down in the passenger seat. Though he'd insisted on stopping just about everywhere, he refused to detour to a beach until it was, as he said, "*The* beach. *Sparkle* Beach."

"We're here," I said, pulling to a stop and applying the parking brake. "You ready?"

Jester stood up and stretched, pushing his front paws out like a fuzzy yoga master.

Berron pulled his messenger bag from behind the seat and leaped out of the car, slamming the door shut, then peering back in through the window. "Hurry up, Zelda!"

I chuckled to myself and unbuckled. "Hold your horses, Gentry."

"Sybelia's not here."

"You know what I mean." I leashed Jester, hopped out, and pulled two cheap beach chairs out of the trunk. The sound of the ocean waves was so close.

Berron took the chairs out of my hands and half walked, half scampered up the sidewalk, past the huge sea grape bushes and picnic tables.

Jester surged after him.

We crested the hill and faced the Atlantic Ocean together.

Berron's hair blew in the wind, just as it should.

"I've never—" He stopped, shook his head. "I've never seen it. Not like this. It's so—"

"Big?" I offered.

"Limitless," he said.

Jester, who had begun sniffing the grass with interest, looked up.

Across the beach, where a low tide ebbed, a group of people were waving.

"That's them!" I said, waving back to Mom, Aunt Belinda, and Luella. I didn't know the rest, but I would soon.

We made our way down the sand-covered wooden stairs. On the last step, we pulled off our shoes. The beach sand was soft and cool like flour with a little butter cut in.

Every step brought us closer to the family we knew and the friends we didn't know yet.

"Are they all magical?" Berron asked quietly.

"Magical or in on it," I replied.

My mom hurried to meet us.

"Mom!" I threw my arms open and she landed with the force of a mother.

Berron stepped back, trying not to get in the way of a family reunion, but was soon hauled in by Aunt Belinda and Mom for hugs so all-encompassing he had to drop the beach chairs.

Aunt Belinda took charge. "You all take a walk or take a load off while we get the grill going," she said, gesturing back to the picnic tables.

"Yes, ma'am," Berron said. He was learning fast. He opened the chairs side by side and dropped his bag into one of them.

I set mine in the other.

"Last one in the sea's a rotten egg!" he said. Then he took off running, pell-mell, toward the waves.

"No fair!" I launched after him, Jester flying alongside.

Berron beat me to the water, but when I got to him, I pushed him so hard he fell over into the waves. He emerged dripping, laughing, and pushing his locks out of his face.

The setting sun gilded the water and made the sky rose-pink on the eastern horizon. The water, cool at first, became a warm bath. A school of tiny silver fish flashed through a wave as it slid into shore. When the wave retreated, colorful periwinkles burrowed into the sand.

Jester pranced through the water and took an experimental nibble of sand.

When we'd had enough of splashing and looking for shells—I found an absolutely perfect whelk—we flopped in the chairs and dug our toes in the sand. Jester stretched out like a fuzzy sphinx and panted with a happy expression.

Berron opened his bag and removed a bottle of Suntan Queen sunscreen, setting it in the sand. Then he took out a wooden case.

"What's that?" I said, recognizing Berron's own woodwork.

He clicked open the clasps and revealed a flamingo-stemmed goblet that caught the remaining sunlight in its details. "Ta-da!"

"Is that... mine? Or did you steal the one from the museum?"

"Yours."

"You can't bring something like that to the beach."

"Why not?"

"Because—"

He stopped moving and looked at me patiently.

"What are you going to do, drink from it?" I said. When he didn't say *no*, I continued. "If you drink from something like that, you're going to start seeing little fairies everywhere."

"I see a big one in the mirror every day."

I put my head in my hand. *Give me strength.* "You don't have anything to put in it."

"That's where you're wrong," he said, fishing in his bag again. "Remember that produce stand I made you stop at?" He pulled out a bottle of fresh-squeezed orange juice wrapped with ice packs. Condensation beaded on the sides.

"Zelda!" my mom called. "Supper's ready!"

"Oh, thank God," I said.

We climbed the wooden stairs back to the picnic area overlooking the beach. One of Luella's friends, dressed all in black, discreetly lit candles with the touch of her finger. A fit and shirtless British man called us over and handed Berron a veggie burger, me a regular burger, and Jester his very own patty. Another friend of Luella's, an energetic woman with curly hair, waved her hands at us and all the water evaporated from our clothes and Jester's fur.

The sun had almost disappeared, but I was warm and dry and safe.

And hungry. The salty air made the food taste even better.

When we were done eating, and all the magical introductions had been made—who had which elemental magic—a beautiful white dog appeared, as if out of nowhere, on the grass.

Jester jumped up, alert, his tail pouf held high.

The two dogs play-bowed, exchanged sniffs, then dashed off together.

"That's Luella's familiar," Aunt Belinda said.

I watched the two dogs dash around: one magical, one *extra*-magical. I might have been biased, but I was pretty sure Jester was the extra-magical one.

Berron had wandered to the edge of the picnic area, where it overlooked the water.

I joined him. In the distance, the Sparkle Beach lighthouse was visible by its rotating light. "Still thirsty?" I said.

He looked at me and raised his eyebrows.

I led the way back to the sand. Took the box out of Berron's bag and undid the clasps. Lifted the glass to catch the first light of the moon and stars.

Berron had the orange juice bottle.

I held out the glass.

He poured.

The sharp scent of citrus made my mouth water. I lifted the glass. The juice flowed over the salt on my lips, like a cocktail, and as I drank, I looked out to the sea.

Limitless.

I raised the glass to Berron and took a second sip, unable to stop from smiling even as my lips curved on the rim of the glass.

"You going to drink it all?" he said.

"I've been known to do things like that," I said. But I handed him the flamingo-stemmed goblet with half the juice still in it.

He caught my gaze, then tossed it back in one go.

Everyone else was making their way back down the stairs, back to the beach. Jester dashed to me, a midnight blur against the white sand.

I scooped him up and smoothed his velvet ears. He sparkled, from the famous sand, and from whatever magic lingered in his soft coat.

And maybe you shouldn't drink orange juice from magic-forged flamingo cups.

Or open long-gone sandwich shops.

Or go on road trips with newly-licensed Gentry.

Or let miniature poodles lick your face by the light of the moon.

But where would be the fun in that?

ALSO BY KATE MOSEMAN

Spells and Sandwiches
Masks and Mirrors
Witch and Wolfhound

Silver Spells
Silver Charms
Silver Dreams
Silver Shadows

A Good Demon Is Hard to Find
A Witch's Work Is Never Done
An Angel in My Teacup

Roller Coaster Romance